Sharp Right to Oblivion

Mark Tournoff

ISBN 0-9545072-1-5

Published by Forestdale Publications

24 Cornwall Court

Wilbury Avenue

Hove

Sussex BN3 6GJ

Design & production co-ordinated by:

Fairways Music

Wadebridge

Cornwall

PL27 6BQ

Printed in England

Chapter 1

A quick glance at his watch suggested to Gareth that there was a flaw in his plan. He had assumed that Helen would turn up at Trevarwick's to buy her sandwich the moment her lunch break began at one o'clock. She should certainly have been there by five past. Throughout the eight years she had spent working at Peterson's Motors the first thing she did at lunchtime was to cross the road and walk down to the baker's. She always went to the same place for her sandwich. Always.

Gareth stood in the doorway and peered up and down the street: there was no sign of her. He checked the time again: it was now gone ten past. A thought crossed his mind. It was traditional at Peterson's to buy cakes for the rest of the staff when it was your birthday. Perhaps she had come down earlier to pick them up and had taken the opportunity to fetch her sandwich then. If so she was probably having lunch in the staff rest room. Damn, why hadn't he thought of that? He decided to hurry over to Peterson's and find her. He did not want her to lose her appetite; the table at Merlin's Steak House was booked for half past one. Helen's parents had rung to say they had arrived about half an hour ago, and Helen's brother Peter and his wife Isobel were almost there too. So typical of his wife's family to arrive early, he reflected.

'Excuse me, have you seen Helen?' Gareth asked the receptionist, whom he didn't recognise.

The girl looked vague.

'I'm a temp,' she explained. 'This is only my second day.'

'She's the bookkeeper. She works upstairs, and her boss Terry said he would let her have the afternoon off so that I could take her out.'

'Ah, yes,' the girl replied, 'I know who Terry is; he's the big boss.' She picked up the phone.

Gareth waited anxiously. It was now 1.15 p.m. If he found Helen straight away, it would take about a quarter of an hour to drive from Bodmin to Wadebridge, and they would just about be on time. He had told the steak house that the booking was an approximate time, so it wouldn't matter to them if they were a few minutes late. He was more concerned about keeping Helen's family sitting around. Helen's mother could be rather impatient.

'He says she went down the back staircase,' the receptionist reported. Gareth looked perplexed. Why had Helen chosen to break with her routine today, of all days? He knew that the back staircase led to the car park at the rear of the building. What if she had driven off somewhere? And to make matters worse, Gareth had discovered that she had left her mobile phone at home on charge. If she had indeed gone somewhere, he would just have to wait for her to come back.

The temp told him how to get through to the back door. He thanked her, and made his way briskly out to the car park. He was relieved to see what looked like Helen's white Fiat in the middle of a row of parked vehicles. He hurried towards a position from where he could see the registration number. Sure enough, it was her car: but there was no sign of Helen. Why on earth had she gone out the back way? There was nothing there. Gareth looked around the car park. He noticed a silver Jaguar starting up in the corner. A man was driving, and the woman in the passenger seat . . . was Helen! He looked again to make sure. Yes, there was no mistaking that mass of ginger hair. Gareth ran in the direction of the vehicle, waving frantically, but they didn't see him. The Jaguar reached the car park exit and turned right, stopping almost immediately to join a queue for the lights at the junction with the main road through Bodmin. Gareth had just passed Helen's Fiat when he gave up the chase. Realising he had the spare keys to the vehicle on his key ring, it occurred to Gareth to set off in pursuit.

As the white Fiat emerged from the car park the lights changed to red, leaving the Jaguar second in the queue of vehicles which had been unable to clear the junction. Gareth joined the back of the queue, and realised there were only about four or five vehicles between them. If he made a dash for it, he might be able to reach them before the lights changed again. On the other hand, if he failed to make it, he might get stranded the wrong side of the lights and lose them. He dithered for some ten seconds, and the opportunity was lost.

Gareth kept an eye on the grey vehicle ahead of him as it turned left onto the main road. The vehicles between them passed through one by one. Directly ahead of him, a red VW Polo was slow to get under way.

4

'Come on, come on,' Gareth muttered. His right hand moved to the centre of the steering column, but self-control restrained him from applying the pressure required to sound the horn. The Polo set off, with the Fiat close on its tail. The lights turned to amber as the vehicles approached, and the leading car only just made it through in time. Gareth was left cursing his luck as he was forced to brake sharply to avoid running a red light.

The Jaguar's journey was not a long one. It travelled less than half a mile before pulling into a parking space outside the Bridge Hotel. As Gareth came along the main road he spotted it from a distance and smiled with relief. He glanced at the clock on the dashboard: it was just gone twenty past one. They would be a little late, but at least he had found her. As he drew level with the parked vehicle he slowed down, glanced to his left, and saw that it was unoccupied. Passing the entrance to the hotel, however, Gareth glimpsed Helen and her companion standing in the foyer. The man was middle-aged and smartly dressed, and he seemed vaguely familiar.

There were no more spaces in the main road, and Gareth had to find a side road in which to park. As he made his way back to the hotel, his attention turned to the question of the purpose of his wife's uncharacteristic deviation from her lunchtime routine, and to the reason for this mysterious liaison. It was so strange that she hadn't mentioned her plans to him. A hideous thought crossed Gareth's mind, but he dismissed it. Indeed, he scolded himself for even contemplating it. No, he assured himself as he reached the entrance to the hotel, Helen would never do that. Not after twenty years of contentment together. Not his Helen.

Instinctively, Gareth followed the signs for the tearoom. His footsteps were silent against the thick crimson carpet which lined the corridor. As he made his way Gareth wondered what to do about Helen's companion. If this was a business encounter, perhaps it could be rearranged. However, if the man were a friend he might wish to come too. It would be easy enough to ring the steak house and ask if they could accommodate a seventh person. He was going to have to call them anyway to let them know of the delay. He hoped the man would not be displeased that the meeting was going to have to be cut short.

The tea room was a large one, but it was virtually empty. Gareth paused by a sign which said, 'Please wait here to be seated'. Spotting Helen and her companion in a far corner, Gareth took a step in their direction.

And then he stopped.

Or rather he froze.

A sickening feeling began to envelop him. There was something about the way they were sitting which gave the game away. They were leaning slightly towards each other in a manner which was almost conspiratorial. And then came the proof, if proof were needed. Slowly thief faces inclined closer until their mouths met . . . and touched . . . and became locked together.

'Can I help you, sir?' said a bright voice from somewhere nearby.

Gareth did not avert his gaze; nevertheless something reminded him that it was essential to retain your dignity whatever the circumstances.

'No,' he replied, hardly able to find the breath to speak.

He paused for a few seconds, before turning to the young waiter.

'Thank you,' he added inconsequently.

Chapter 2

'Well, Gareth, it's most unfortunate that we're not going to get to see Helen,' declared Celia, as she handed the menu back to the waiter. Aware that her son-in-law was reluctant to return her gaze, she turned to her husband in a way which suggested that she was counting on him to voice his agreement. However, Miles Vaughan shrugged his shoulders and remained silent. Celia was undeterred:

'I know you had the best of intentions, but I do wish you had thought it through more carefully. We've come a long way just for this, that's all I'm saying.'

Gareth was still struggling to think of a reply when Helen's brother Peter chimed in:

'Couldn't you have waited for Helen to come back, and then brought her over here? At least we would have got to see her that way.'

'I didn't think of that.'

'Who was this friend she went for lunch with, anyway?' Celia wanted to know.

Gareth tried not to show his feelings.

'I don't know,' he said quietly.

Miles looked at his son-in-law curiously.

'Are you sure you're all right?'

'Yes, yes I'm fine, just . . . you know . . . disappointed.'

Miles looked unconvinced. Gareth was concerned that his father-in-law might pursue the matter further. However, the arrival of the first course brought about a timely interruption. A subdued atmosphere prevailed as the meal progressed. Gareth tried to focus his gaze on anything other than the empty seat opposite him. Between courses he excused himself and headed for the washroom. Here he allowed himself to succumb to his distress for a few minutes.

The immediate aftermath of the awful moment was a blur. Whereas others would have sought confrontation, Gareth's reaction was to get

7

away from the scene. He did not recall doing so, but he must have walked back through the hotel, along the street, and around the corner. He had made it as far as the car before his world began to disintegrate around him. His eyes clouded over, and an unfamiliar tension crept over him, leaving his body rigid.

As he sat rooted to the driver's seat a shrill purring sound startled him. He fumbled in his jacket pocket, took out his mobile phone, and blinked at the screen. He recognised the number as that of his mother-in-law.

'Gareth, is there any sign of her yet?' Celia had demanded to know. There was no way Gareth was going to tell her what he had just witnessed. It wasn't just that he was reluctant to admit his humiliation. Despite everything, he felt a duty to protect Helen from the ill feeling he knew she would have to face from her family if the truth were known.

'She's . . . well, it seems she's gone to lunch with a friend,' he stammered, a wave of pain enveloping him as he spoke. Celia had tut-tutted in dismay before bringing the conversation to a swift conclusion.

Reluctantly, Gareth summoned the strength to return to the table. There was a sudden hush as he entered the room. Gareth felt certain that they had been discussing his plight. Peter's wife Isobel appeared to lift a finger to her lips. She smiled uneasily at Gareth as he took his seat between her and Celia. The remainder of the meal took on an almost farcical character. Attempts at jovial conversation were launched sporadically, Miles being the chief instigator, but each seemed to splutter to a halt. Beneath the smiley surface an undercurrent of discomfort was apparent to all present. Before they had finished the after-dinner coffees Gareth seized the chance to ask for the bill.

'I'm going to pay for everything,' he asserted. 'It's my way of apologising for Helen's absence.'

'No, no, let's split it evenly,' Miles intervened, reaching for his wallet.

Celia was shaking her head.

'I think it's only reasonable under the circumstances to accept Gareth's offer.' Her husband looked set to protest, but she got in first. 'After all, we have all come a very long way.'

Gareth did not need reminding that he had always thought of her as a difficult woman.

'I insist that you let me pay,' he declared, forcing a smile as he looked around the group.

The moment of release could not come soon enough. It was nearly four o'clock before Gareth was able to allow his hand to fall back to his side, the final farewell waves having been exchanged. As he got back into Helen's Fiat Gareth looked forlornly at the untouched birthday cake which Isobel had placed on the back seat, beside two bags containing unopened presents and cards. With a heavy heart he drove back to Bodmin, stopping off at his own car to unload before returning the Fiat to Peterson's. He parked the vehicle in the space from which he had taken it. As he got out of the car he found himself looking around to see whether there was any sign of the silver Jaguar. It dawned on him that from now on he might be haunted by the image of that vehicle and its driver, and for the first time his grief was superseded by an uneasiness bordering on fear.

Chapter 3

'Hello, Mr Bell. How are you? Are you well?' sang a voice to Gareth's left as he walked down the path towards the front door. He looked across the fence which divided the front lawn, in the direction from which the cheerful sound had come. At first he saw nothing. Suddenly from behind the bush in the middle of the lawn a teddy bear's head popped up. Then a small oval-shaped face peered round the side of the bush, grinning cheekily in a way which revealed an untidy arrangement of front teeth.

'Hello Megan. I'm okay, thank you. How are you?'

'I'm okay. Teddy's okay. Jimmy's okay. Mummy's okay. Everybody's okay.'

'That's good,' Gareth replied absent-mindedly, rummaging in his jacket pocket for his key.

Megan lay down on her back in the grass and cradled the teddy bear to her chest. She smiled unfalteringly towards her neighbour as she watched him pass through the doorway.

Inside the cottage all was quiet. Normally the tranquillity would have suited Gareth's temperament. Today, however, the silence was oppressive. A glance at the birdcage in the corner of the lounge revealed that Joey was asleep, his head tucked into his back. Gareth noticed Helen's mobile phone, still plugged into the charger, on the table nearby. How different the course of the day's events might have been if she had taken it with her as usual, he reflected. He might have got through to her before her liaison, and he would still have been in the dark about it. Gareth wondered how long the affair had been going on. He remembered he had noticed that Helen had been receiving a lot of text messages recently, and had not always been very forthcoming about their contents. Deciding to investigate, Gareth went over to the table and stood there for a moment; then with trembling fingers he disconnected the mobile phone from the charger.

Scrolling through the inbox, he examined the list of senders' names of the messages which had been saved there. His own name was there, along with her mum, Terry the boss, her friend Julie, and then . . . Harvey . . .

then her mum again . . . then Harvey again . . . and again. Gareth paused there, knowing that he had heard that name recently, but unable to remember where or when. He opened the message:

'Hi gorgeous, table booked for eight thirty. Stay sexy for me.' The message was dated 19-07-02, exactly a week beforehand. Gareth recalled that Helen had told him she was 'eating out with Julie' that evening. He checked another message:

'You bet I noticed you straight away. It was your hair I guess. And that blue dress you had on . . . so stylish!' Gareth was in no doubt about which dress it was. He had helped her choose it. And the only occasion she had worn it was at the barbecue his brother Andrew had put on in acknowledgment of the longest day of the year. Gareth's mind went back to that Friday evening. It had been a sizzling day, culminating in a glorious evening. Andrew's back garden sloped down towards Polzeath beach, and at around ten o'clock the guests had gazed intently to the west as the sun had slipped into the sea.

And now Gareth remembered who Harvey was: Andrew had introduced him as being his new neighbour, revealing that he was a singer with the pop group *Kosmos*, a fact which immediately made the newcomer of greater interest to Helen than to him. For this reason it had not surprised Gareth that his wife had spent such a long time in conversation with the man, while he had joined the group discussing the forthcoming World Cup semi-finals. So this was the fateful occasion.

Gareth went back to the list of saved messages, and selected the remaining entry attributed to Harvey. As he did so, he recognised a sound from outside the cottage. He turned and looked out of the front window, just as the noise of the engine stopped. After a moment Helen's freckly face became visible over the roof of the Fiat. As she came through the gate she looked towards the lounge window. Helen was beaming. But her smile was not prompted by the sight of her husband. Rather, she was grinning mischievously in a way which reflected the contents of her daydreams. Halfway down the path she paused, just as Gareth had done earlier, distracted by the same quirky innocence which still overflowing from the other side of the hedge. Megan's intervention prevented Helen from discovering that her husband would be unable to return the smile, and allowed Gareth time to examine the text:

11

'You were just wonderful last night. Your taste lingers on my lips, and my mind's eye is full of images of you. I can't wait to be with you again.'

The front door opened.

'I'm home . . . Goodness! Are these for me?'

Helen bent down and began to examine the contents of the bags which Gareth had placed on the floor in the hallway near the bottom of the stairs. Long gingery strands toppled over her shoulders and dangled over the bags, obscuring her face completely. Gareth turned away, unable to look at her any longer, a lump forming in his throat.

'Ah, how sweet! But when did you see Mum and Dad?' She continued her investigations as she spoke. 'And Peter and Isobel?'

Helen glanced towards her husband, puzzled at the lack of a response.

'Gareth!'

She stood up, passed through the open door of the lounge, and stared in his direction.

'Is something wrong?'

Still nothing. She moved towards him, reached up, and placed her left hand on his shoulder. He shook it off and stepped away to the corner of the lounge, close to the birdcage. The sound of voices had woken the budgie. Joey began to chirp merrily, one dark little eye looking diagonally up at Gareth, as if contemplating his owner's distress.

'Have I done something?' She tried to get round in front of him, but he turned in the opposite direction and in a moment was in the kitchen. She followed him as far as the doorway.

'Leave me alone!' he declared, finding the strength to speak, but still not able to face her.

Helen's jaw dropped as the reality dawned on her . . . he knew. She had no idea how he knew, only that he must have found out somehow. There could be no other explanation for his behaviour. This was the moment she had been dreading. She looked at the floor as the first pangs of guilt struck her. Then another disturbing thought came to her: this discovery and the mysterious arrival of the presents might be related in some way. Did her family know too?

12

Helen remained where she was, clueless as to what to say or do. She watched as Gareth stood over the kitchen sink, his back to her, staring out of the window. For perhaps half a minute the only sound was that of the tap which Gareth had failed to turn off properly that morning, dripping into the bowl in which the crockery he had used at breakfast had been left to soak. Then another noise was heard, a series of shrill beeps – three short ones, followed by three long ones, then three short ones again – reminiscent of the distress signal in Morse code. Helen realised that Gareth was clutching her mobile phone in his right hand.

He must have seen the messages from Harvey.

And now another one was coming through!

She made a move towards him, but Gareth had already confirmed his suspicions. Without letting go of the phone he plunged his right hand into the washing-up bowl.

'No!' Helen snapped, but it was too late. After a moment Gareth relented. Keeping his back turned to her, he thrust the handset onto the draining board. Helen retrieved it; although it had been thoroughly drenched, it was still working. She turned and carried the phone through into the lounge, then checked that Gareth had not followed her before examining the message:

'Nearly at the airport. Missing you terribly already. Will text again from Munich. 39 days and I'll be back forever! Stay in bloom, little flower!'

Helen recoiled at the reminder of her lover's forthcoming thirty-nine-day absence. She had noted the band's entire schedule in her diary, so she would be able to work out where he was at any given time. She knew the first few dates by heart: Munich tomorrow night, then Berlin Sunday and Monday, then Basle . . . Helen hoped that the mobile phone network would extend to all the destinations; she really didn't want to be out of touch with him at all. She scrolled through to reply, then thought better of it. She really needed to clear the air with Gareth, and find out whether anyone else had made the same discovery. Returning to the kitchen doorway, she saw that her husband was still in the same place – the only difference was that he was no longer staring out of the window, instead he was standing with his head bowed. There was something bizarre about his posture - so much so that Helen found herself stifling a nervous giggle.

Gareth looked round, and the glimpse he caught of her suggested she was smiling. Surely she wasn't mocking him, not at this awful moment? Unable to look at her for more than a second, he went back to staring out of the kitchen window, towards the array of colourful plants and flowers which his wife had nurtured.

Helen remained in the doorway, gazing helplessly at the same disconsolate sight she had contemplated shortly beforehand, feeling the same pangs of guilt she had experienced then. She had to do something to break this up.

'Gareth, we need to talk,' she said eventually. 'I'll wait in the lounge until you're ready.'

She turned and took a seat on the sofa. She waited for perhaps a minute, but nothing happened. Eventually her anxiety to reply to her lover got the better of her. She looked again at Harvey's message. Helen realised how much her hands were trembling as she began pressing the keys:

'Darling, Gareth knows about us. Oh hell, what do I do? I'll call as soon as I can. She paused, then added: *Safe journey, my love.'*

She had just pressed 'Send' when Gareth came into the room. Ignoring the empty space on the sofa, he sat down in the armchair on the other side of the table. Helen found herself too overcome with shame to look her husband in the face. Gareth did not want to make eye contact either; he sat on the edge of the seat, and buried his head in his hands, his elbows resting on his knees.

For some minutes the only sounds were the gentle ticking of the clock which sat on the mantelpiece over the hearth, and the occasional chirp from the cage in the corner. Even Joey's mutterings were subdued, as though he had somehow sensed that all was not well. Eventually, Gareth broke the silence:

'Why?' he asked quietly.

His voice was so plaintive, so uncomprehending, that Helen had to swallow hard as she struggled to keep hold of her emotions. At length she attempted an answer:

'It's . . . that...there's something very strong . . .between Harvey and me . . . something I can't honestly say I've ever felt for you . . . it's . . . I don't

14

know . . . a sort of chemistry . . .it's just there . . .it's so obvious . . . it's irresistible . . .'

She paused, and momentarily dared to glance across at her husband. She wished she hadn't. His face was bright red, his eyes and nose totally concealed behind cupped hands.

'It was there right from the beginning . . . Harvey felt it straight away too . . . I've never known anything like it before with anyone else,' Helen continued. Her voice betrayed a note of excitement, despite the situation. The hint of fervour was not lost on Gareth. Allowing his fingers to open a little, he peered incredulously towards her as she spoke. She paused again; Gareth raised his head and allowed his fingers to run down his face until they reached his chin, dragging teardrops with them as they went. Helen risked another look, and seeing the extent of his distress felt overcome with guilt. Unable to go on speaking, she waited for Gareth to say something. It was not long before he found his voice:

'But how can you let something like that affect our happiness?'

Helen shook her head slowly.

'I'm not happy. I haven't been for years. Haven't you noticed? You've never thought to ask, have you? You've just taken it for granted that because you were happy I must be too. Well, I just can't go on playing the part of the dutiful wife any longer. I've got the chance of having something real with Harvey, and I intend to take it.'

'So you're leaving me?'

Helen looked uncomfortable. She had begun to see this as inevitable, but was not ready to confront anything so final yet. Everything had happened so quickly. After a pause, she attempted a reply:

'I'm not sure how things are going to work out. I don't know whether I'm going to be able to carry on living here or not. Harvey's just gone on tour, and won't be back until September, which gives us a chance to think things through and come to some decisions. I do know things won't be the same between us again.'

Gareth had buried his face in his hands once more, and was silent. The absence of eye contact encouraged Helen to look towards him again. The need to give vent to her exasperation suddenly proved too much for her:

'Why don't you say something? What's the matter with you? Shout and scream at me if you want, call me anything you like, throw things at me if you must, but for heaven's sake don't just sit there!'

For a moment Gareth remained impassive. A voice in his head was reminding him of the importance of keeping control of one's feelings: 'Dignity, my son, dignity at all times.' However Helen's outburst spurred him into action, and he became lucid:

'I'm too shocked to even think straight. Until a few hours ago I hadn't a care in the world, not the slightest idea that anything was wrong. If you weren't happy, you should have said so, instead of pretending. We could have worked through our problems. But no, you had to go and take the matter into your own hands, without so much as giving me a chance to put things right.' He shook his head disgustedly, before continuing, more calmly: 'I still don't know what's wrong. So how come you aren't happy?'

Helen sighed. She looked down at the table between them as she began her reply:

'It's several things. I know it's not your fault, but I've never really been able to get past the fact that we couldn't have children.'

Gareth felt dismayed that she had brought up the subject once again. Several years had gone by since she had mentioned the matter, leaving him with the impression that she had overcome her disappointment.

'I can only apologise so many times for not being able to give you what you wanted,' he said.

'I know,' she responded. 'It's not just that, though. There's also the fact that you're too easily pleased. You're quite content to stay as just a teacher all your life. You could so easily have become a head teacher by now. At least you could have made progress. But look what happened last summer. That time there was a vacancy for deputy head. You didn't even try for it. And I didn't even know about it until after the deadline for applying had passed, otherwise I would have got you to go for it.'

'I wasn't hiding it from you, I assure you.'

'I know that. You just weren't interested in it, so you wouldn't have thought to mention it. That's your trouble; you're too complacent. You're just not ambitious. Whereas Harvey . . . '- she hesitated, knowing the comparison was going to be hurtful, but feeling she had to make it anyway - 'Harvey makes things happen.'

Gareth looked enquiringly at her, the pain showing in his face.

'You know, *Kosmos* haven't always been famous. It took years of perseverance. But Harvey believed in what he was doing. He knew he could write quality songs, and that they are a really talented group. So he kept on going until they made it. I admire that in a man.'

Gareth shrugged his shoulders.

'Well, actually, I'm proud of being "just a teacher", as you put it. I feel that it was what I was meant to do. You see, when you guide a class through several years, as I have, you get to know them really well, and you contribute towards their development as people, in a way which is really rewarding. Anyway, what's the point of getting another job that I don't want just because it would be better paid and more prestigious?'

Helen made no reply; she was not entirely convinced, but found it difficult to contradict him.

'Is that all, or was there something else?' Gareth continued.

Helen swallowed heavily. There was indeed something else, and it was going to be the hardest thing of all to talk about. She sighed loudly as if to warn him that something unpalatable was coming his way. Gareth looked suitably anxious.

'No, that's not all,' she began softly. 'It's . . . well, you know things have never been that good between us . . . you know . . . '. She glanced across at him, to see whether he was following her, but his expression suggested he needed to hear more. 'I mean in bed,' she said finally. Their eyes met, and she could not escape noticing how forlorn he looked. She felt the need to continue, if only to put an end to the matter. 'Whereas . . . '

Helen's voice tailed off for a moment. Gareth's face was screwed up in pain. In reality she had said all she needed to confirm the awful truth. Gareth had clung to the hope that fidelity might have restrained her, or even if it hadn't, that perhaps her relationship with Harvey had not yet reached that stage. That single word proved that a comparison had been

17

made, and an unfavourable one at that. The rest of the sentence was almost superfluous; nevertheless she decided to complete it: '. . . Harvey is very good . . . very skilled . . . things between us just fell into place immediately.'

Helen dared not look now; indeed she turned her head away, in the direction of the front window, in order to be sure that she did not catch a glimpse of her husband. But there was no way she could prevent the muffled sound of his sobbing from reaching her ears.

A gentle tap on the front door took her attention away from Gareth's grief. Another, slightly louder, followed immediately. Helen rose and peeked through the window; a moment later she was in the hallway.

'Happy birthday to you! Happy birthday to you! Happy birthday Auntie Helen! Happy birthday to you!'

'Thank you, Megan,' she said hoarsely, forcing a smile as she accepted a small box wrapped in purple paper. 'I'm sorry, I can't ask you in.'

And she closed the door on the little girl's puzzled face.

Chapter 4

It was dusk when Gareth came back into the kitchen. He had been sitting on the wooden seat near the bottom of the garden, his gaze focused mainly on the jagged stone path which ran past the bench. Ants crawled about their business; butterflies fluttered, bees hummed. But Gareth was oblivious to their endeavours; such was the extent of his pain and fear that his mind could accommodate little apart from his cogitations on this newfound disarray.

Inside the cottage Helen had opened her presents: a porcelain figure of a ballerina from her parents, some books and CDs from Peter and Isobel, and a mug with her name on from Megan. She had changed into some jeans and a top, and was sitting in front of the television, not really taking in the episode of *Friends* which was being shown, but preferring the sound of human voices to the silence which would otherwise prevail. Hearing Gareth shut the back door behind him, she waited until her husband came through into the lounge.

After a few seconds he appeared in the doorway:

'Do you want anything to eat?' Helen tried to sound warm and sympathetic.

Gareth shook his head. Food was not a matter of concern to him. Rather he wanted to implement the decision he had made without further delay.

'Come and sit down,' she invited him, but again he declined her offer.

'You really should have something to eat,' she observed.

'No thanks,' he replied absent-mindedly.

Gareth went across to the small table near the lounge door and picked up the phone. Helen waited to hear him speak, but after about thirty seconds he replaced the receiver. She looked over her shoulder towards him, and once again the hurt in his eyes was inescapable.

'Who were you calling?'

He hesitated before replying:

'Andrew.'

She waited for him to elaborate, but no explanation was forthcoming. A noisy advert prompted Helen to cut the sound of the television. In the corner Joey seemed to take this as his cue to stop chattering. Helen could not wait any longer for an answer to her question. Summoning up her courage she again looked towards her husband, who was still hovering close to the phone:

'When did you see my family?'

Gareth flinched at the reminder of the occasion. Then he told her, as succinctly as he could, what had transpired that lunchtime. Where others might have seized the opportunity to aggravate the offender's sense of guilt, Gareth described the whole ordeal in a matter-of-fact way: the surprise he had planned, her non-appearance at Trevarwick's, the moment of truth at the hotel, and the celebration of her birthday in her absence. Despite the sensitivity inherent in Gareth's explanation more weight was added to the growing burden of shame with which Helen found herself lumbered. Though an apology seemed pointless, she endeavoured to make one anyway. Gareth said nothing in response, for in reality there was nothing meaningful which could have been said. Helen felt relieved that her family had not been made aware of her affair, either before the meal or through anything Gareth had imparted; she was grateful to him for that. Although she was coming to the conclusion that it was inevitable that she would have to tell them, at least it would fall to her to choose the time and the manner of the confession.

Gareth made a move towards the phone, but as he did so it rang. He soon passed her the receiver: it was her mother. They had just got back to Dorchester, after a fraught journey through the heavy traffic which was a regular feature of a Friday evening at this time of year. Helen thanked her mother for the present and apologised profusely for her absence at lunchtime. So who was the friend she had been seeing, Celia wanted to know? There was a suggestion of resentment in her voice. Helen hesitated, aware of her husband's presence. 'A very nice man I met recently,' she replied cagily. Celia didn't question her further, but there was an uneasiness about the rest of the conversation from which Helen concluded that her mother was suspicious.

Helen felt reluctant to get involved in another potentially difficult conversation with her family that evening. She guessed that Peter and Isobel would still be on their way home, since the journey back to Basingstoke would take even longer, so she called their home number and left a message of thanks. No sooner had she replaced the receiver than Gareth picked it up. Helen watched as he waited once more for a response, lingering for perhaps a minute, before giving up again. This time her curiosity got the better of her:

'Why are you calling Andrew?'

'I'm going to go and stay with him, if he agrees, which I'm sure he will.'

Helen looked taken aback.

'I can't stay here with you, not under the circumstances,' he continued. 'I don't think I'll ever be able to sleep beside you again. I don't even know whether I'll ever be able to spend another night under the same roof as you. I've been thinking about it out in the garden, and that's what I've decided.'

Helen continued to stare at him, until he turned away from her; he still found it hard to look her in the eye. Although she wanted to protest against his conclusion, she felt too shocked to formulate a response. Moreover, she knew that while it took him some time to make up his mind, once he had done so it was almost impossible to get him to change it. His strength of resolve was something that she admired in him. Turning to face forwards, Helen tried to find something on which to focus her gaze, hoping to distract herself momentarily from the gravity of the consequences of her husband's announcement. Her endeavours were in vain: she could tell her eyes were clouding over, and her throat was tightening. She covered her face, as Gareth had done earlier, in an attempt to fight it off. Helen viewed shedding tears as a sign of weakness, and rarely gave way to her emotions. Now, however, the pressure was overwhelming, and she began to sob. Her sadness at the situation, and the knowledge that her actions were responsible for bringing it about, combined with her trepidation at the thought of what might follow. Helen wondered how she, or anyone else, would ever make up for her husband's grief and sense of betrayal. How could she have brought such distress on someone with whom she had shared her entire adult life? It wasn't that she no longer cared for Gareth; it was just that the relationship

21

had long since run its course, at least as far as she was concerned. It wasn't like a genuine marriage any more; it was more of an alliance based on habit, a mere convenience. If only he could have recognised that as clearly as she had. Helen had hoped that maybe he had secretly tired of their union, that perhaps in reality it had become stale for him too. If so it would not have come as too harsh a blow to learn that she had moved on; however it was evident from his reaction that this was clearly not the case.

The sound of footsteps above made Helen aware that Gareth had left the room and gone upstairs. She heard him open the wardrobe in their bedroom, and there was a dull thud as a suitcase hit the floor. Helen knew that if she wanted to try to stop him, it was now or never. 'Oh hell,' she said aloud, dabbing her eyes with her handkerchief in an attempt to make herself presentable to speak to him. Then she shook her head in dismay. This was not how she had envisaged things turning out. She had hoped to have the opportunity to find the moment to explain the position to him in such a way as to gain his understanding and acceptance, possibly even to reach an amicable agreement as to what to do. She was still contemplating whether to approach Gareth, and what she might say to him if she did, when a digital melody began to play, causing her heart to miss a beat. Helen grabbed her mobile phone from the table in front of her, and checked the screen. Sure enough, the words '*Harvey mobile*' had been called up from the handset's memory, and with a sigh of relief she accepted the call.

Gareth struggled to fasten the suitcase which he had crammed with clothes and shoes. He made no attempt to go about this in an orderly manner, he simply aimed to take as much as he could, in order to equip himself to get by for as long as possible without having to return to the cottage. Shirts that had been carefully ironed by Helen were clumsily folded and squeezed into a corner of the suitcase. In reality Gareth found it difficult to focus his mind on even the fairly straightforward task of packing, such was his preoccupation with his predicament, and he nearly forgot to take toiletries with him. Realising his omission just as he had won the battle to zip up the case, Gareth opened it again, flung a couple of pullovers across the bedroom, and headed for the bathroom. Passing the top of the staircase, he became aware that Helen was on the phone. He could just about make out what she was saying, and it was soon apparent to him from the tone of her voice that she must be speaking to her lover.

Though this realisation cut into the depths of his being, he found himself stopped in his tracks and compelled to listen:

'Aha . . . yes, I know where you mean . . . and you're sure they'll be there . . . aha. Oh, Harvey, I just don't know what to say . . . are you really sure about this? It's just . . . I am, I am if you are . . . you're right, it does make a lot more sense . . . listen, I'll talk to him. I'll talk to him and then ring you back. You won't be going to bed just yet, will you? Okay, look, you know I love you, but I love you even more for this . . . No, don't worry, I'll be alright . . . No, it's okay, he could never hurt anyone . . . he's too kind for his own good, really . . . Okay, look I'll speak to you very shortly . . . okay . . . love you . . . bye . . . bye.'

As Helen rang off she heard Gareth's footsteps on the stairs. She knew how sound travelled in the cottage and was alarmed to think that he must have heard at least some of what she had said. There would be no time to consider what to say to him. Not that it mattered so much now; the real harm had already been done. She would simply have to come straight out with it, and tell him what Harvey had suggested, and that she intended to go along with it.

As Gareth came into the lounge, Helen got to her feet, and for the first time since she had come home he was able to look her in the face for more than an instant. He had heard enough to know that something fresh was afoot, and curiosity had taken hold of him, enabling him to overlook for the moment the discomfort which the very sight of his wife now inflicted upon him. He could see that she was a little uneasy about telling him something - however he felt confident that whatever it was she couldn't hurt him any more than she already had, so he decided to encourage her to come out with it.

'Well?' he began. 'What is it you want to talk to me about?'

Helen looked away, and then sank back down on the sofa.

'Come and sit down,' she invited him softly, indicating the chair opposite.

Gareth stood his ground.

'Just tell me!' he replied. His voice was quiet, but firm.

'Harvey's come up with a better idea,' she responded. Summoning up her nerve, she looked across at him, before continuing:

'You stay here. I'll go and stay at Harvey's house.'

'How can you? You said he's just gone away. Will you be able to get in there?'

Helen suddenly felt her frustration overcome her:

'Oh, for heaven's sake, Gareth, say what you think. Can't you at least say whether it matters to you whether I go or not? Yes? No? Does it bother you either way? Any normal person would have some sort of gut reaction! Only you could go straight to the practicalities of the situation! That's you're trouble, you're too dispassionate''

'Oh really, that's what you think. Actually that's the opposite of the truth.'

'Well, you could have fooled me!'

'Look, just because I don't lose my temper, or curse and swear like a lot of people would, it doesn't mean I don't care, okay? Anyway, if you want my gut reaction, I'll give it to you. I think you should go. That's what's going to happen anyway, isn't it? Yes, go now, this evening if you can. *That's* why I wanted to know whether you could get in there.'

Helen hesitated to respond. She was taken aback by her husband's unequivocal response, which evoked mixed feelings in her. On the one hand she was relieved that he had offered no resistance to her suggestion, on the other she couldn't entirely avoid a sense of disappointment that he had not found it in him to plead with her to stay.

'All right,' she said finally, turning towards him again, 'I'll go this evening. And yes, I can get in there. Harvey's told me where to get hold of a spare key.' She paused for thought, forcing herself to concentrate on the task in hand. 'I'll just take what I need for tonight, and I'll pick up the rest of my things gradually. Don't worry, I won't take anything which belonged to us both without talking to you first.'

Gareth looked her squarely in the eyes, then replied:

'Take what you like; it doesn't matter. They're just things. They're of no consequence.' He paused before concluding: 'Everything that matters has gone already.'

He spoke calmly, in a measured voice, eliminating any suggestion in her mind that he might be responding irrationally. Then he passed behind the sofa, into the kitchen, and on once more into the back garden. There was no longer any need to seek a place in which to ruminate, however. This time he was merely looking for sanctuary – taking refuge from the sight of his wife preparing to leave the home they had shared for nineteen years and ten months.

Chapter 5

Gareth sat up in bed with a start, and then felt around on the bed to his right, hoping vainly that his mind had been playing tricks on him. A glance at the clock on the bedside table told him that he had not been asleep long, less than an hour in fact; however, this had proved enough for him to dream in a manner which reflected his malaise. Surrounded by wriggling fish, he imagined himself entangled in an enormous net, from which he had been struggling to free himself when he awoke, warm with sweat, his heart pounding.

Gareth went over to the window and drew back the curtains, allowing a hint of light from the street lamp outside to enter the room. As he lay back down, he thought he could hear the sound of someone sobbing. He listened intently, unsure as to whether he might be imagining it. At length he worked out that what he could hear was coming from the other half of the building. The sobs were those of little Megan. Strange, he thought, she was normally such a happy child. Although Gareth was a heavy sleeper himself, Helen was not, and he felt sure that if she had ever heard Megan crying in the night she would have mentioned it to him. It seemed to him that the little girl's tears were in some way connected with his own grief. He told himself that this was unlikely, even illogical, but there was something about the whimpering which seemed to reinforce this impression. He just couldn't work out what it was.

Some minutes elapsed, and still the plaintive sounds reached Gareth's ears. Almost involuntarily, he clambered out of bed and made his way to the top of the stairs, so that he could hear more clearly. Gareth had often heard children crying in school, usually as a result of a playground tumble or an infantile squabble. These sounds were altogether different; they were somehow more profound than that, far more like the sounds of an adult crying - the way Helen might have sounded if she had ever surrendered her resolve to shed tears in total privacy.

So that was it.

His curiosity satisfied, Gareth felt a sudden urge to stem the tide of his little neighbour's lament:

'Hush! Don't cry, Megan, don't cry' he murmured, and to his surprise, within a few seconds the crying stopped. Gareth felt certain that he had spoken too softly for the little girl to hear him through the wall. It must have been coincidence, he concluded. Returning to bed, he wondered once more what had prompted Megan's tears. It was possible, of course, that either she or her mother had looked out into the dusky half-light, spotted Helen loading her car and driving away, and realised what was going on. And if so, it was likely that this would have reminded Megan of the occasion, the previous summer, when her own father had left home and never returned. Yes, Gareth decided, that was the most likely explanation, although he doubted whether he would have the opportunity to find out for sure.

Back in the king-sized bed, which now seemed ridiculously ample, he became aware of a fresh source of vexation. For some reason he hadn't noticed it when he had first tried to sleep, but now he could smell Helen's scent lingering on the sheets. He turned over to face away from her side of the bed, hoping to put some distance between his nostrils and the source of the aroma, but still traces of 'Youth Dew' reached him. Gareth was too tired to set about changing the sheets in the middle of the night. He decided to put up with it for now, and see to that tomorrow. Burying his nose in the pillow, he caught a glimpse through the gloom of the book on the bedside table which he used as a journal. It had been his practice ever since his first days away from home to create some sort of record of each day. He would log any events in his own life, in the lives of people he knew, or perhaps in the news, which would give the day uniqueness in his memory. It was a method of lending each day of his life a character of its own. He had found using an ordinary diary too restrictive. Sometimes he would want to write several paragraphs. More often a couple of sentences sufficed. Occasionally, when something particularly distressing had occurred, a solitary comment was all he could manage. Gareth recalled the last occasion when he had struggled to write anything: September 11th 2001.

The notorious events of that day were hard enough to bear for anyone who had witnessed the terrifying images. However, they had a greater poignancy for Gareth than for most people, especially because the planes had been crashed intentionally. Gareth's mind was taken back inescapably to New Zealand, to 1989, and to a light aircraft which was being flown by his uncle Les.

Gareth had a hazy recollection of his uncle, compiled from a patchwork of incidents from his early teenage days. He remembered Les as being uncommunicative, except on the several occasions when his character had been radically transformed by alcohol.

Gareth recalled the last time he had seen Leslie before he had emigrated. It was New Year's Day, 1974. Les had been drinking from a pint glass. Gareth could see that it wasn't beer he was knocking back and had asked him to identify the mystery substance. 'This,' said Les slowly, looking intensely into the eyes of the youngster, 'is blood'. Les looked deadly serious. 'Try some,' he went on, holding the glass out towards his nephew, 'only don't spill it. It's very, very unlucky.' Gareth sniffed the port, and with a smile he reached out to take the glass, but Les snatched it back from him.

'Don't tease the lad, Les,' Gareth's mother had appealed to her brother, 'he's done nothing to you.' Les turned and looked icily at her.

'Give him time,' he declared. 'He hasn't been around as long as the rest of you.'

'You know, I'm worried about you, Les,' said Gareth's father. 'You're getting paranoid!'

'What's paranoid?' Gareth had wanted to know.

'You mean you don't know?' sneered Les. He beckoned his nephew closer. 'It's an album,' he whispered, 'by Black Sabbath.'

Gareth was about to sit back. 'Bloody good album!' Les shrieked in his ear. Gareth nudged his uncle's glass as he took fright.

Les surveyed the red splodge on the cream-coloured carpet. He shook his head solemnly. 'Very unlucky,' he muttered, before looking up and fixing his eyes on Gareth: 'Very unlucky indeed!'

Fifteen years later, Gareth's parents had decided to celebrate his father's retirement by travelling around New Zealand. Les had been flying them from Auckland to Wellington when his Cessna had crashed into the summit of a hill. All three had been killed instantly. The crash had been attributed to pilot error, the weather being unexceptional and the plane deemed free of mechanical defect. It had come to light that Les had been drinking heavily the previous evening. Gareth and Andrew were both convinced that Les had deliberately taken his own life and those of their parents.

And so it was inevitable that the sight of the burning buildings on that dreadful day the previous autumn should bring back grim memories. The fact that there was an altogether different form of cynicism underlying the events of September 2001 was irrelevant. A single word was all that Gareth had managed to enter that day, yet it summed up the reason for his inability to write more. It read simply: 'Traumatised.'

As for Friday 26th July 2002, a day when so much had happened, a day which had now rolled into Saturday 27th July, there was still no entry in the journal. Now, as he peered through the gloom at the dark-blue cover of the book, this omission seemed to add to his woes, as though his neglect of it represented failure on his part. He closed his eyes in an effort to shut it out, but the image of the journal remained. Gareth found himself muttering aloud:

'All right!' He clawed at the bedside table, until he had the book in his grasp. 'I'll put something, just to keep you happy.' He fumbled for the switch on the small bedside lamp. The pale glow it provided would suffice for a short entry. And it would indeed be a short entry. He opened the book at the point where he had left off the previous evening.

His mood on Thursday 25th had been cheerful and optimistic. He had been looking forward to springing the surprise, and to seeing the joy on Helen's face as she saw her family unexpectedly. The entry reflected his uncertainty as to whether the present he had chosen for her was appropriate. Now he realised that he would never know. Any thought of giving Helen her gift had been lost in the turmoil of the evening, and she had left without it. Being reminded of how upbeat he had been the previous day proved too much for Gareth, and he again felt tears welling up inside him. As he looked down on the space he was intending to fill, the first teardrop plopped down onto the paper. Others followed, until the page was sprinkled with droplets of moisture, and seemed too soggy to write on. And then it dawned on Gareth to leave the journal this way, as a means of reflecting the unhappiness of which this day marked the onset. There was no need to add anything - the tear-stained page said it all. So he simply replaced the book on the table and put out the light.

Chapter 6

As Andrew dialled his brother's number he looked out across the grass he had just finished cutting and wondered whether he would have another opportunity to make use of his new barbecue set before the season ended. It would be a pity not to let anyone else have the benefit of seeing the many flowers which had come into full bloom since the previous occasion. Andrew cast his mind back to that June evening. Unlike Gareth, he had paid some attention to the first conversation between Helen and Harvey and had observed the rapport between them. He had noticed that Helen had seemed fascinated by Harvey, indeed almost spellbound by him. Andrew couldn't have described exactly why, but it was as though he had seen a new side of Helen in the short time she had spent talking to Harvey that evening. He had been left feeling relieved that he had no reason to think that their paths would cross again. Even so he was anxious for his brother's well-being, and had been intending to have a word with him as soon as an opportunity arose. He decided that if she wasn't around he might do this now.

Gareth approached the phone reluctantly. Most phone calls were for Helen: she had a number of friends who sometimes rang for no particular reason. Gareth had no wish to discuss the previous day's events with any of Helen's family or friends. On the other hand he didn't want to mislead them by pretending all was well. He resolved to say that she wasn't around at the moment and that he would ask her to call them back. The phone had been ringing for about half a minute before he finally picked up the receiver. Whoever it was, they were persistent, he reflected.

Normally he would have greeted the caller with a cheery 'Hello, Bodmin 516513'. On this occasion he uttered only the first word, and there was a hoarseness about his voice from which anyone who knew him well would have been able to tell that something was wrong.

'Gareth, what's up?'

There was a moment of silence while Gareth hesitated. Here was the one person in the world who might be able to provide him with some comfort and support, yet Gareth did not know how to begin to break the awful news.

'Come on, man, spit it out!' Andrew urged him. In keeping with his role as manager of a haulage firm, Gareth's brother knew how to speak in an authoritative manner without being over-bearing.

'It's Helen,' Gareth began finally.

He had already said enough for Andrew to have some idea what had happened. Andrew had always liked Helen, but had never completely trusted her. He had gained the impression that she was increasingly looking for something better than she had, and remembered that Helen had once confessed that she had 'a ruthless streak'. Andrew had perceived a lack of fulfilment in her, and could not help feeling that she held Gareth at least partly responsible for this.

'She's left me,' Gareth went on after some seconds.

Andrew felt unable to feign astonishment. He stood, motionless, his gaze fixed on the view from his lounge window: the sloping lawn with its rose bushes, the beach below, packed with sunbathers and surfers, and in the distance the Atlantic Ocean towards which the sun was already beginning to make its descent. Just beyond the bottom of the garden ran a path which led down to the beach. The track was at its narrowest at this point, and a young couple on their way down stood aside just by the back gate in order to allow the passage of a family coming towards them. This caught Andrew's eye without holding his attention; his mind was focused on what he could possibly say to console his brother.

'I see,' he replied eventually. 'I'm really sorry to hear that, Gareth.'

Andrew waited for his brother to continue. However, Gareth was particularly reluctant to explain where his wife had gone: on the one hand because the admission that there was someone else involved exacerbated the indignity of the situation, on the other because he didn't want his brother to feel bad about the fact that it was owing to him that they had been introduced.

'You don't sound surprised,' Gareth commented finally. Before his brother could answer, a thought crossed his mind:

'You didn't know, did you?'

'No, no, of course not, it's just that, well, last time I saw Helen, she seemed . . . 'He paused, choosing his words carefully. 'Well, she seemed rather distant, as though she wasn't happy.'

Gareth felt crestfallen that the issue of Helen's discontentment had not been lost on his brother, whereas his own confidence in his wife's happiness had been unshakeable.

Andrew hesitated to mention his impression of the conversation between Helen and Harvey. He was reluctant to aggravate his brother's plight by introducing the suggestion that his wife might have been susceptible to another man's advances. He carried on staring out of the window - still only partially aware of what his eyes were taking in. Suddenly, however, that all changed. A solitary figure now occupied the space vacated by the young couple. Andrew's face fell at the realisation that his brother's wife, the subject of the heart-rending conversation in which he was involved, was even now standing at the foot of his garden. Open-mouthed, he waited for her to reach for the latch to open the garden gate and let herself in. But Helen just stood there for a few seconds, as those before her had done, while three lads carrying surfboards came down past her. Andrew thought that she looked towards him momentarily; he was unsure whether she actually saw him, but it was obvious now that she had not come to visit him.

He watched in disbelief as she stepped back onto the path and carried on up the slope. Andrew moved sideways in order to keep her in his view. She went past his immediate neighbour's back gate, and was soon within yards of the rear entrance to Harvey's property.

The telephone wire was at full stretch: Andrew needed to let go of the receiver in order to obtain confirmation of what he feared. Although there was only one sensible explanation for Helen's movements, he found it impossible to accept. He had to be sure that he had not jumped to the wrong conclusion.

'Just a second, Gareth,' he murmured, trying to sound calm. Leaving the receiver on a chair he edged further towards the window, until he reached a point where he could just see Helen's head above the hedge which bordered Harvey's back garden. Andrew prayed that she would keep going up the path. For a moment it seemed that his prayer had been answered; Helen carried on past Harvey's back gate. But Andrew's sigh of relief was short-lived. His sister-in-law stopped, realised she had overshot, and turned back.

Andrew looked on in dismay as she fumbled with the unfamiliar latch. He did not stop to watch her pass through the gate: he had seen enough. He returned to the receiver and picked it up. 'Sorry about that,' he began, eager to confirm to his brother that he was back on the end of the line. However, he found himself incapable of continuing. He could not give a truthful explanation for his momentary absence; nor could he find it in himself to dream up some excuse. What was more, Helen had inadvertently supplied the answer to the question he might otherwise have asked. Now he felt the need to cling to the possibility that Gareth was unaware of his wife's whereabouts, and did not want to have this slender hope dashed by asking for more details. And so, just as Gareth was waiting for a hint of reassurance, Andrew found himself worse than useless, too stunned by what he had witnessed to be even remotely helpful. Conscious of the need to say something - anything - he managed to ask Gareth what he had in mind for the rest of the evening.

'Evening?' came the reply. Gareth had been roused suddenly by the sound of the phone, and had mistaken the dusky half-light for the break of the day, a day which in reality he had all but missed.

'Yes, that's right, it's nearly eight o'clock,' Andrew affirmed, grateful of the chance to put his brother straight, even in the most insignificant of ways, yet at the same time alarmed at the implications of Gareth's confusion.

Another pause followed as Gareth took on board the consequences of this latest revelation. The conversation had become extremely disjointed. Finally he replied that he had no plans: he would simply be staying where he was.

'Do you want me to come over?'

'No . . . sorry, no thanks.'

In reality, Gareth badly wanted his brother's company, but a mute irresistible pressure held him back, forcing him to decline. Some message conveyed to him long ago dictated that he had to find his own salvation. To accept the offer would have been tantamount to an admission of weakness. Gareth even managed to feign levity as he observed that it would make a pleasant change to spend a Saturday evening at home, alone.

Reluctantly, Andrew accepted his brother's decision. Inferring from it that Gareth might consider the prospect of further discussion of the situation a strain, he hastily brought the conversation to a conclusion with a promise to check on his well-being the following day. It did not take Andrew long to realise that he should have been more insistent, and within minutes he dialled his brother's number again. Initially he was surprised that the call went unanswered, but then it dawned on him that Gareth had no reason to think he would be calling again and was unlikely to be prepared to break the bad news to anyone else that evening. The ringing ceased, and Andrew held the receiver away from his ear until Helen's voice had finished inviting him to leave a message.

'Gareth, if you change your mind, I won't be going to bed early. Just let me know, okay?'

Even as he put the receiver down, Andrew was beginning to reflect on the turn of events. Although it was absurd to think that he might have foreseen the outcome, he could not help cursing himself for having invited Harvey to the barbecue. He remembered the moment well. Andrew had been to the store at the bottom of the hill, and had forgotten to buy milk. Realising he would not have enough to provide for his cereal the next morning, he had decided to go back to the store. On his second return journey, he had used the rear path, for no other reason than that of variety. It was then that he had met Harvey coming towards him.

Andrew had taken the opportunity to enquire how his new neighbour was settling in, and a short conversation had followed, concluding with a mention of the barbecue. Even though Harvey would not have known anyone else, his response was unequivocal, accompanied by a broad grin and a wink. It was as though even then he was counting on finding someone who would succumb to his charms.

It was bizarre, thought Andrew, as he opened his drinks cabinet, how trivial quirks of fate could radically change the course of a lifetime. If the weather had been as bad as forecast that day in New Zealand, his uncle might have been forced to abandon his plan to fly his parents to Wellington. If it were not for his own forgetfulness, and his determination to adhere to his breakfast routine, his brother and sister-in-law would still be together this evening. Andrew acknowledged that this would not have ensured a happy outcome for Gareth. If it had not been Harvey it might soon have been someone else. But at least there would have been a chance that events would have turned out differently. Now, it seemed, that chance was gone.

As Andrew took the first gulp of brandy he had poured he was struck by the depth of his reflections. He was grappling with matters on the very fringes of his mental capacity. How was it, he asked himself, that the hand of destiny was dealt with such cruel randomness? Was there really any logic in it all, any underlying sense of natural justice that ensured that all would be well in the end? Poor Gareth; whatever he might have done, or not done, he certainly didn't deserve this. Why let it happen to him, when other people were given second, third, or fourth chances? Take Lennie from the depot, for instance, whose wife had consistently taken him back after his affairs; he would only have had himself to blame if she had sent him packing.

Andrew took another swig, without being distracted from his reflections. There were times when nothing made sense, while on other occasions when events seemed to work out for the best in the end. He recalled how, aged eighteen, he had been unceremoniously dumped by his first girlfriend, Elaine from Petersfield. She had given no explanation at the time, but soon afterwards he thought he had heard her friend Joanne say that 'she had gone back to Lewes'. How naive he had been, puzzling over the notion of a previously unknown association with a quaint town near Brighton! Later somebody had pointed out the alternative explanation of Joanne's remark, and soon afterwards a letter bearing her Hampshire address served as confirmation that indeed she had not moved away. The letter made no mention of the rekindling of an old flame, merely enquired as to Andrew's health and expressed the hope that they might remain friends. For a long time Andrew had been unable to forgive Elaine, and the letter remained unanswered. As adulthood bestowed upon him deeper understanding and greater tolerance, he had relented, and had renewed contact with her, to the extent of accepting her company in the presence of mutual friends. When he moved to the West Country it was at Elaine's suggestion that he had visited the library and obtained details of local activities, and it was through the choral society he had subsequently joined that he had met Cassie. Dear, muddle-headed Cassie! She could be seen as his reward for forgiving Elaine - or perhaps as his punishment for not having forgiven her sooner! Andrew chuckled as he emptied his brandy glass, and then felt peeved at the thought that he had allowed himself a moment of humour at such a time. Wherever this flight of introspection was going, it had better lead to something that would be of use to his younger brother.

He got up and returned to the cabinet. There would be no holding back this evening. He was in shock and needed something to deaden the sensation. The clock in his lounge chimed the half-hour. Outside the gloom was gathering, but Andrew did not stop to put on a light before flopping onto the settee. Now where was he? Ah yes, Cassie. She could hardly be described as the love of his life, nor did he think she would speak of him as being the love of hers. She had flitted in and out of his life ever since he had taken the first step onto the managerial ladder as a Delivery Office Manager in Bideford. Their relationship had been on and off enough times to lose count: it must have been at least twenty, probably nearer thirty, over the course of a decade. At the moment it was 'off', but he knew better than to presume that it was over for good, just as when it was 'on' he was loath to believe that it would last. But the experience had taught him how to avoid allowing his state of mind to be determined by how things stood between them. He had settled onto a plateau, on which he had found a measure of contentment, a sort of emotional no-man's-land somewhere between happiness and unhappiness, and nobody was going to evict him from it. Not even Cassie. He was confident that he was invulnerable to anything any woman could do to him. If it really were over this time, then he would look back in years to come and say 'so be it'. And if nobody else ever came along, there were more than enough other things in life to sustain him. His career had blossomed. He had reached a point where he had attained an enviable degree of autonomy, yet he had avoided being burdened by an excessive level of responsibility. If the most recent inspection by the South West Area Coordinator was to be believed he was 'liked and respected by all at the depot'. He could not progress any further without accepting an unwelcome relocation. At least his own circumstances were such that he would be free to support Gareth in his hour of need.

And so Andrew's thoughts returned to his brother. What troubled him most was the certainty that Gareth's experiences had not endowed him with a similar degree of independence. His brother's life with Helen had instilled in him a sense of security which had turned out to be false. Gareth was devoted to his wife, in a way that was obvious for all to see. And it was equally evident that such devotion could not be retracted, or conveniently redirected towards another, more appreciative, recipient. That was how it seemed to Andrew, as the stupor which was enveloping him rendered him lucid, or clouded his understanding - he never knew for sure which it was. So what could he do to alleviate Gareth's suffering? For the moment, nothing more than be there for him whenever he was needed. But as time began to heal the wounds he would endeavour to elevate him to the same level of immunity from the opposite sex on which he himself had already found repose.

Satisfied with his plan, Andrew headed once more for the drinks cabinet, but found that he had already emptied the brandy bottle on his previous visit. He grinned at this discovery, knowing that when he was deep in thought he often lost track of his actions. Only the other day he had returned to the kitchen to do the washing up only to find that he had already completed the task. Then Andrew realised that if Gareth did call back he would have had too much to drink and would not be able to drive over to his brother's house. Never mind, he thought, if necessary he would ring for a taxi. Failing that he would ask one of the neighbours. 'I'll even bang on bloody Harvey's door and get him to take me over there, if necessary,' he said to himself out loud. And then he recalled that when their paths had last crossed Harvey had mentioned that he was going on a tour shortly. Realising that Helen must be there on her own, Andrew wondered whether there might be anything he could do, or say to Helen. He would have to discuss it with Gareth first of course. Perhaps he wouldn't want her back now. Perhaps even *his* tolerance had been exhausted. After considering this possibility for a moment, Andrew dismissed it with a rueful smile. Whatever Gareth might be feeling at the moment, it certainly would not affect his love for her. Given time, he was sure to want her back...

Chapter 7

The garden at dusk would normally have had a gentle, soothing effect, thought Gareth as he closed the kitchen door and felt for the light switch. During term time, it was a good place to recover from a hard day at school. At this time of year he would often take his journal outside with him and spend longer than usual considering how to summarise the day. Very occasionally, Helen would come and sit with him, if she had something in particular she wanted to talk about, and if there was nothing interesting on the television. Gareth would tease her, saying that she only came out if she wanted him to do something for her. 'Well, actually there is something . . .' she would reply, and he would invariably agree to her request, sometimes readily, sometimes after a little persuasion. This evening, he had to face the fact that there was no chance that she would join him, and the absence of this possibility made the experience of being there burdensome rather than consoling. Yet if the garden was lonely, the cottage was almost forbidding; the silence that lay in wait for him was quite eerie.

Once inside the murky lounge Gareth felt a shudder: Helen wasn't there, yet she was everywhere - and so was Harvey. Somehow the darkness seemed to increase the vividness of Gareth's imagination, and images that had been troubling him while he was outside loomed with alarming clarity. They were starting to torment him now. He remembered Harvey's face all too well: the deep tan which gave him the appearance of a continental, the neatly groomed dark hair, the turquoise eyes which provided such a striking contrast. There was no denying he was a man who was extremely attractive to women, the sort of person who stood out in a crowd. And now this man was with Helen . . . his beloved Helen . . . Gareth's mind's eye involuntarily turned its attention to his wife . . . he could see her in that dress, the blue one she wore that fateful evening at Andrew's. He could see her from behind, see all that wonderful copper-coloured hair, see how it fell some way below her shoulders, but did not prevent the dress from showing off much of her back. Enough of her body was visible to show that it was beautiful; she was slender, shapely and well proportioned. But, to Gareth at least, her skin was her outstanding feature. It was unusual in its colouring, a sort of cross between cream and orange, and it blended remarkably with her mass of hair. He imagined himself up close now, right by her, looking down on those freckly shoulders. And then she turned to face him, and he saw the twinkle in her eyes, and became mesmerised by an aura so bright that it would bring light to a darkened room. And then he realised the unbearable truth. Helen was facing him all right, but it wasn't him she was seeing, it was Harvey. Even though she was looking right at him, her attention was elsewhere, and her eyes were still seeing another man, her new man, Harvey *Newman*. The irony of the name struck Gareth for the first time, but he did not stop to dwell on it. He had this image before him, so bold and clear it was awe-inspiring, and it was up to him to toy with it. He could do whatever he liked with it. Helen might have taken her body away from him, but she couldn't erase his memories. A single bolt of lightning struck her image from behind, setting it alight. 'Come here,' he commanded. At once she was drawn to him, opening her arms and enveloping him. And now his head was lost in all that hair once more, his eyes were closed and his face was alive as he savoured every golden strand. His hands were on her back now, gently fondling her skin, relishing the smoothness of her flesh. A finger strayed under one of the thin straps which held her dress in place, and he ran it up to the top of her shoulders, then looped it round and tugged it to one side until it dropped a few inches down her arm. She was breathing heavily, almost panting, and she gasped as he moistened her nape with a circular movement of his tongue, simultaneously freeing the other strap until the dress began to drop. It slithered downwards, and she wriggled slightly to aid its descent, but as she breathed out it stuck on her breasts. He watched as she held her breath for some seconds, teasing him for what seemed an eternity, making him anticipate his delirium. He could see the two protrusions through the blue material, and even as he waited eagerly for the moment of their exposure he noticed that they were more erect than usual. Fantasy, it seemed, could be even better than reality.

It occurred to him that the images he was seeing were not simply the product of fantasy, but reflected what had actually happened that evening in June. He had noticed the gleam in her eye at Polzeath, but had wrongly attributed it to the beauty of the sunset. He had undressed her later that evening, and had noticed the desire in those gorgeous rosebud nipples, and he had believed her when she said that it was because she felt so sexy in that dress. They had made love that night, and a couple more times the

40

following week, but not since then. It had not been uncommon for her to go through short phases of frigidity over the years, and then come out of it, so he had thought nothing of it. As the image of Helen faded into oblivion he wondered how he could possibly have been so blind to reality.

It was half past three in the morning when Gareth discovered himself curled up on the sofa. He was shivering, and his back and forehead were moist with sweat. The harrowing experiences which disturbed his sleep had been forgotten the moment he woke up, as his attention returned to the nightmare which his waking life had suddenly become. His first action had been to feel the covers of the furniture around him, groping for something familiar, grappling in the dark for a means of establishing his whereabouts. He had satisfied himself that he was indeed in his own home, albeit in the lounge when he would normally have been in the bedroom. But that was not the only reason he was groping around. He was like the proverbial drowning man, clutching at straws, seizing the slightest possibility that it wasn't really happening. Perhaps he was hoping he would magically come across Helen's form lying beside him. In reality his hand had initially made contact with the floor, on which it had discovered his journal. He could not remember what he had written in it the previous evening, although he knew he had put something. Gareth sat bolt upright, suddenly recollecting the lucidity of the previous evening's images, realising at the same time that something was happening to him over which he apparently had no control - and he had to admit it was frightening. On Friday evening it had seemed so obvious that he and Helen had to part straight away. Now he wasn't so sure. If there was a chance of reconciliation, he had squandered it. Did he want her back? Yesterday afternoon, the answer would have been in the negative. But after last night . . . Of course he wanted her back. She was his Helen, his heartbeat, his lifeblood. He would never be the same without her. Grabbing the journal, Gareth hurried to the kitchen. Here it was light enough to see what he had written while he was in the garden. He flicked through the pages anxiously, sensing that maybe there was a glimmer of hope in what he had put. It wasn't an unreasonable suggestion. The garden was a place of inspiration, after all. Trembling fingers batted the sheets of paper backwards and forwards. Finally he found what he was looking for. The entry was indeed short, one of the shortest ever;

nevertheless it was sufficient to provide an answer. It stated simply: *First Day of Solitude.*

Chapter 8

The bell rang again as Gareth reached the bottom of the staircase. He felt more than a little uneasy about opening the front door. Having stripped away the sheets to which Helen's scent still clung for two days after her last contact with them, he had been lying on the mattress, feeling drained. The absence of any attempt to remake the bed was not down to laziness; rather his preoccupation was such that he had no motivation to consider the task, still less the concentration required to perform it. It was a nuisance that whoever was at the door seemed aware that someone was at home. Gareth knew it couldn't be Andrew. His brother had phoned as promised, and they had finished speaking a few minutes before. The most likely candidate was Megan. Or could it be that Helen had decided it was no longer appropriate to use her key?

Gareth recognised the faces he saw, but had no idea why they were there. He could see the concern in their expressions as they looked at him. Was it really that obvious? Jarrod and Rowena exchanged glances as Gareth stared at them. Behind them he could see that Megan's head was just visible over the wooden fence. She was looking in their direction, nibbling at the tip of her index finger. Even she looked troubled.

'Us still goin' Cat'n'Fiddle, boy?' Jarrod asked. Gareth looked blank.

'I fixed it with Helen during the week,' Rowena explained.

'Oh,' said Gareth, realising an explanation would be required. The couple were Helen's friends originally: Rowena used to be Terry's personal assistant at Peterson's. They had got together three or four times in recent months. Although they were pleasant company, Gareth sometimes struggled to understand Jarrod's accent, particularly after he had downed a few pints of Doom Bar. The prospect of spending an evening trying to make conversation under the circumstances did not appeal at all. Gareth decided to get his announcement over with quickly:

'I'm afraid Helen's left me.' He looked at the ground as he spoke.

'Left 'ee?' Jarrod asked loudly.

'Yes.' Gareth looked at him momentarily, glanced likewise at Rowena, and then focused his gaze on Megan, who was still watching intently.

'Sorry about that, Gareth,' said Rowena. She sounded much less surprised than Jarrod. 'Can we do anything?'

'No, nothing, thanks.'

'Will 'ee still come with us?' Jarrod wanted to know. 'Might do 'ee good.'

'No, I wouldn't be much company, I'm afraid.'

'Don't worry 'bout that. We'll cheer 'ee up. That's what friends be for.'

'I'm sorry, Jarrod, I really don't feel up to it.'

'You sure?'

'Jarrod!' Rowena interrupted. 'Leave Gareth be!'

He accepted defeat with a nod. Rowena took him by the arm and began to steer him away.

'Gareth, tell us if you need anything,' she concluded.

'Thanks, Rowena, I'll do that.'

Gareth breathed a sigh of relief as he watched them leave. If Jarrod had persisted, he might have been talked into tagging along, in order not to offend them. The more he thought about it, the more the idea of sitting in a pub with a couple whom he had only ever met with Helen seemed altogether unbearable; it would just have served to reinforce his consciousness of her absence. Gareth couldn't help feeling annoyed that Helen had forgotten to cancel the arrangements. As he shut the front door behind him, vaguely aware that little Megan was still eyeing him curiously, he wondered what other surprises might lie in store. He went to the kitchen and checked the calendar behind the door, but there were no engagements of which he was unaware. Indeed nothing had been written against that day to indicate that a drink had been organised. It was so unlike Helen to forget, though . . . It struck Gareth that there had been no calls from any of Helen's family or friends since Friday evening, whereas normally there would have been several. Presumably she had contacted them to tell them she had moved out. Why, then, had she overlooked Jarrod and Rowena, with whom she had apparently made arrangements during the week? It occurred to Gareth that she might have left them in the dark deliberately, in the knowledge that they would turn up that evening. But why? Maybe she hoped he would spend the evening with them in order to take his mind off things. Or was there some ulterior motive? Did she perhaps want him to do his share of breaking the news? Or was she so taken up with Harvey that she had simply forgotten?

The fact that he felt so bewildered simply added to Gareth's woes. He realised how little he knew about the woman with whom he had lived for so long, to the point that he couldn't say whether she was acting out of kindness, forgetfulness, or obduracy. He wanted to get to the bottom of the matter. He decided to take up the issue with her next time she came in to pick up her belongings.

Absent-mindedly, Gareth slotted a couple of slices of bread into the toaster, then returned to the lounge to top up Joey's seed bowls. Looking after the budgie had always been his task. Gareth had originally bought Joey as a present for Helen, at a time when she had been feeling particularly low about the fact that they were childless. However, she had taken little interest in the bird, and Gareth now regarded him as his own pet.

Dusk was beginning to fall now, and as on the previous evening it seemed to emphasise Gareth's solitude. He searched in vain for something on the television to take his mind off things. The smell of burning toast drew him back to the kitchen. A glance was enough for him to decide that both slices were inedible, and he tossed them in the bin. Opening the fridge he surveyed the contents. On the bottom shelf was a single bottle of Blue Nun – it was Helen's favourite, and for this reason he hesitated to take it. He was trying not to think about her, but all around him were reminders of her: ornaments she had put in place to give character to their home, framed photos of happier times, books she had read. Even his CD collection was mostly made up of presents she had given him over the years. Now he was confronted with the wine he had bought for the quiet evening together that he had anticipated would follow the surprise birthday meal. He had finished the last of the whisky the previous night, and now it was a choice between Blue Nun and abstinence. He paused for a few moments, then snatched the bottle from the fridge, and opened it hurriedly. Before he knew it he was out in the back garden, a large glass in one hand, his journal in the other. Seated on the bench he held the glass up to his lips; then he shook his head in disapproval. Blue Nun was too sweet for his palate. Chardonnay was his favourite - Australian or Chilean preferably. Never mind, he thought, as he raised the glass again; this evening he was drinking purely for effect, and it would be the last time he would have to drink sweet wine. Tomorrow he would fill the fridge and the wine rack with his own choices. When he lowered the glass again it was half empty, and it was not long before he needed to return to the kitchen for a top-up. Even a large glass seemed inadequate. A distant recollection offered the solution. 'Uncle Les,' he muttered aloud. He reached up to the cupboard above the sink and took out the tankard that was normally reserved for guests who preferred lager. As he tipped the rest of the bottle into the tankard, he managed a smile. He would not have felt at liberty to do that if Helen had been around. Now he was free to do as he wished. He raised the tankard aloft and gulped down a quarter of a pint. Again, he shook his head. 'Disgusting stuff,' he commented. He checked the label: 'Ugh! Nine per cent! No wonder!' He wandered into the lounge, and dodging the furniture, made his way to the far corner. 'Want some, Joey?' he enquired. The bird looked curiously at him. 'It's got a little bit more taste than water . . . not a lot, though, just a little . . . '. There was no reply, not a single chirp. 'No? Okay, suit yourself!' And he made for the garden . . .

There was still enough light to write something in the journal:

'Drank wine from a beer glass. A triumph! Used up the last of Helen's Blue Nun. It was a way of saying goodbye, I suppose.'

That was sufficient. He snapped the journal shut, then sniggered: 'A triumph!' he proclaimed. 'A pathetic, meaningless triumph, to be sure, but still a triumph.' Gareth discovered that he was staring at the empty bottle, which had been left for no apparent reason on the garden path. He could feel the frustration welling up inside him. There was nobody to see his malaise now, nobody to take a dim view of a display of emotion. Gareth pounced on the bottle, raised it high in the air, then hurled it down onto the stone in front of him, with such force that one of the resulting fragments caught him on the chin. Then he fell to his knees, and tumbled forwards until he was lying flat on the ground, giggling mischievously.

Some minutes later he sat up. Some faint noise behind him, a sniff perhaps, suggested to him that he was not entirely alone. A look over his shoulder confirmed his suspicions. Gareth felt embarrassed to see a small egg-shaped face peering at him over the hedge. He rummaged around for something to say, but he need not have bothered. Megan had her own comment to make. Without averting her gaze, she said simply:

46

'I don't like Auntie Helen any more.'

Chapter 9

The milkman paused as he reached the front door. He had brought three bottles with him. Usually it would be either two or three pints on a Monday morning; there would be a note left to let him know which. But this morning was different; the doorstep was bare - no note, no empty bottles either. Although he was unsure what might lie behind this occurrence he knew what to do about it. There were customers who sometimes forgot, and his policy in such instances was to err on the side of generosity. What puzzled him was that the lady with the long ginger hair was one of those who never forgot. He shrugged his shoulders, placed the three bottles in the usual spot, and headed back down the path. Before he could reach the gate, another surprise came his way. A white Fiat came to a stop just behind his float, and the lady whom he knew as Mrs Bell got out. He waited for her to notice him, but she walked towards the cottage with her head down, her eyes to the ground. Clearly she was preoccupied with something, an observation which heightened his sense of intrigue.

'Morning to you' he began, as she finally looked up. 'How much do you want today?'

She seemed unable to focus her attention on the question:

'Oh, er, one pint should be enough.' She passed by him and carried on towards the cottage. Realising the need to retrieve the surplus, he followed her down the path. She was turning the key in the door as he bent to pick up the bottles. Suddenly she added:

'In fact, make it one pint every time from now on.'

Helen glanced over her shoulder, looked down at him momentarily, and knew from his expression that he had understood. She entered the cottage without saying anything further, and as she closed the door quietly she congratulated herself on the subtlety of her message.

She had made plenty of explanations over the weekend: to her parents, to her brother, to her friends, and in a letter to her sister Patricia in America. The conversation with her mother had been the hardest. She knew in advance what the response would be, but the words were still ringing in her ears: 'You made your vows, you should have stuck to them - you can't go changing your mind just because someone more suitable has come along.' There was no point in arguing her case. Her mother's standards were absolute: what she had done was wrong and that was all there was to it. Peter had been more ready to listen and attempt to understand her situation, but she sensed his disapproval. Prompted by Isobel, he had called back and asked whether she thought they should contact Gareth: she had replied that he would find talking about it difficult and that it would be better to leave him alone.

In keeping with her natural tendency towards secrecy and discretion, Helen had previously refrained from confiding in anyone about the affair, except for her long-standing friend Julie, a social worker from Camelford. On hearing that she had left the cottage, Julie had offered her some reassurance, saying that it was better that she was with the man she loved than to be stuck in a marriage that wasn't working. She had also advised her to go through the process of telling people and get it off her mind as soon as possible. Now that she had left the cottage it was only a matter of time before her other friends found out anyway. It was preferable that the news came from her and not via the grapevine. Nevertheless Helen had found the task stressful, and would be glad when she reached the bottom of the list.

Helen began to fill the holdall she was carrying with books and ornaments, trying to give some thought to the question of whether she could claim them as entirely hers. But other matters were preying on her mind. Harvey's phone had rung a couple of times, and the caller had hung up when she had answered. Another time she had missed a call because she had been in the bath, and had heard a message being left by a woman in what she thought was Spanish, a language in which she knew Harvey had written songs. She had played the message back several times without being able to make any sense of it. But she didn't need to understand its content to recognise that the woman had a sexy voice and an affectionate tone.

Helen had sent Harvey several texts on Saturday, but he had not replied until Sunday. He had been taken up with work all day and the Munich gig in the evening. When he did reply he had said simply:

'Munich diabolical. Really cheesed off. Sorry no contact. Speak to you later. H xx'

The text had only served to aggravate Helen's suspicions. Harvey had such charisma that it would be easy for him to find a woman to spend the night with, if that was what he wanted. Could she really expect a man with his high sex drive to remain faithful to her for the duration of a seven-week-long tour? And even if he was telling the truth, how often did he sink into such low moods? Helen was beginning to realise that there was still much she didn't know about her new love. One thing was for certain: he was very unlike Gareth. As Helen moved quietly around the lounge, she wondered why all the exciting men were dangerous to be with, whereas the safe ones were altogether too boring. If only it were possible to take the attractive elements of one man and combine them with the appealing features of another. Ideally she would like to match Harvey's virility and ambition with Gareth's reliability and thoughtfulness.

Helen had just finished collecting ornaments when she heard her husband's footsteps on the stairs. She stayed where she was, her back to the doorway, anxiety causing her to tighten her grip on the holdall and the paperweight she was clutching in her other hand. She had hoped to get away from the house before Gareth got up. Normally during the school holidays he would lie in until around nine o'clock. Helen had been too absorbed in her problems to think what she might say if she did see him. Not wanting to reveal her trepidation, she took a deep breath, and then glanced over her shoulder at him. Wanting to appear casual, she tried to say hello, but the word stuck in her throat.

Gareth took hold of her wrist in an attempt to get her to look him in the face. The paperweight tumbled out of her hand and fell to the floor, narrowly missing Helen's foot. She gasped, and Gareth let go of her arm. She flashed him an angry look, then bent to retrieve the paperweight. It had been a present from a late aunt and was a favourite ornament. The carpet had cushioned its fall and a quick examination showed that it was intact.

'You could have broken my foot!'

He hesitated: he was reluctant to apologise before going on the offensive, but he couldn't bring himself to ignore her point altogether.

'Well, I'm sorry about that. But you were trying to hide from me. What are you up to? What's going on?'

She was facing him now, trying to make sense of the suspicious look he was giving her.

'I don't know what you're talking about.'

'About last night.'

'What about it?'

'Why didn't you stop Jarrod and Rowena from coming round here?'

She looked mystified. He was almost certain that her bewilderment was genuine, but the lingering doubt showed in his face.

'They were supposed to be coming next Sunday. I was going to put them off, but I hadn't got round to it yet. If they came last night, then they must have got the date wrong.'

He went silent, and she turned away from him and looked towards the mantelpiece, pretending to resume her contemplation of the ornaments. She was trying to find the words to express what was irritating her. His continued proximity vexed her further, and she moved away to Joey's corner of the room. She looked down into his cage while continuing to ponder. As she stared the bird shook himself, ruffling his feathers in a way which seemed to reflect her own mood. Suddenly she became lucid, and she turned to confront Gareth:

'So what did you think I had in mind?'

He shrugged his shoulders. His head was drooping, and he was looking down at the floor, his eyes half closed, the strain etched on his face. If he had not been so provocative, she thought, she might have found it within her to comfort him.

'I'm not sure. It's just that it's so unlike you to forget. It just felt as though you had some ulterior motive . . .'

'Like what?'

'I thought maybe you were forcing me to do my share of telling people. I guessed you would be finding that difficult . . .'

'You're right I'm finding it difficult!' Exasperation was causing her to raise her voice now. 'Every time I tell someone I wonder whether they'll

51

speak to me again. But I'm taking it all on, to save causing you any more pain than I already have. And what do I get in return? Instead of recognising that there must have been some sort of mistake you accuse me of having some devious plan in mind. You've just made it very clear to me, Gareth, that I was right to leave you. All this time we've spent together, and you still don't really know me at all.'

Her outburst had caused him to look plaintively at her. Helen couldn't bring herself to return his gaze. She turned and headed for the door.

'That's just what I've been thinking,' he called after her, stopping her in her tracks. 'I don't know you. You're not the person I thought you were at all.'

Helen remained where she was, still facing the doorway. She spoke calmly, in a measured voice:

'I'll be coming in very early during the week to fetch my things. Please will you stay upstairs until after I've gone. And don't try to call me at all. I'll be in touch with you when I'm ready.'

She made her exit briskly, slamming the cottage door behind her.

Chapter 10

The back garden was quiet and still, and the sun was blazing in an otherwise vacant sky: a tortoise-shell butterfly settled on the low privet hedge dividing the properties. It was a summer's day to relish, a day when families would take snapshots of picnics in the park, when golfers would celebrate low scores fostered by the ideal conditions, when teenagers would meet at discos and experience their first kiss. Elsewhere there would be happiness, but in this tiny part of Bodmin the roses bloomed unnoticed.

As Megan lay flat on the grass she was faced with a choice of pathetic sights. Resting her head on her elbow she glanced from one sufferer to another, deriving no pleasure from either yet mesmerised by each. For the one nearer to her the pain was nearly over. She wished she could tell it she was sorry, that she hadn't meant to hurt it, that if it hadn't sneaked up on her from behind like that and frightened her then she wouldn't have swatted it. But there was nothing she could say to it that would change anything, nor was there anything she could do for it. The bee was crippled, and its legs, which were pedalling the air in desperation, were beginning to flail more slowly.

On the other side of the hedge, Mr Bell was lying flat on his back on the wooden seat. Did he know she was watching him? She thought not. He had been fidgeting for some time, shaking his head and rubbing his hands together, but now he seemed to be punching the air, as though he could see someone she couldn't. Perhaps he too had an imaginary friend, and they had had a big row. She whispered this to Jimmy, and he agreed.

A glance back at the bee confirmed that its battle for survival was over. Megan wished it safe entry into the kingdom of dead insects, and concentrated on her neighbour's plight. She saw him struggle into a sitting position, pick up what looked a like an exercise book, and begin to scribble intently. Curiosity was getting the better of her. She went over to the hedge and began to watch him through a gap in the top. He didn't notice. She knew from her mother that Auntie Helen had gone off in a huff on Friday evening, but she wanted to know where and why, and she sensed an opportunity to find out. Perhaps Mr Bell would tell her, if she asked nicely. Not wanting to interrupt him, she waited patiently for some minutes. Suddenly he looked up:

'You made me jump.'

'Sorry, Mr Bell.'

Gareth wondered how long she had been standing there, and whether she had witnessed his preparation for the confrontation he did not expect to materialise. It felt strange, looking up at the sky but seeing instead the face of his foe. He wanted to rid himself of this image, an image which had somehow become clearer in his mind as he had recalled it repeatedly over the past few days. Gareth had rediscovered hatred, an emotion to which he had become a stranger since he had been bullied at school. He had not been involved in a fight since he was eleven, and his childhood scraps had been more like wrestling matches than punch-ups, but now he had remembered what it was like to want to really hit someone. Gareth had imagined himself delivering a series of powerful blows to his adversary's nose, causing it to become bulbous and misshapen, giving those suave features a ridiculous appearance. As he allowed his hand to drop to his side a feeling of deep shame took over. True, Harvey was a man who had brought unhappiness into his life in order to further his own pleasure. Nevertheless he was a human being, and Gareth reminded himself that he had no right to wish destruction on him like this. If the opportunity ever arose to strike back in this manner, he would not actually take it - but that wasn't the point. Gareth was aware that if he heard that some form of harm had befallen Harvey, he would consider it a cause for celebration. That this should be so was a source of revulsion to Gareth, who had always thought of himself – and been considered by others – as a kind soul. But love was such a strong emotion, and desire such a powerful driving force, that he couldn't help feeling the way he did. He suspected that most people would have felt the same way, but this was scant consolation: he didn't feel comfortable with such malevolent thoughts.

'You were having a play fight just now, weren't you?' observed Megan, who was now standing, looking over the hedge.

'Yes, you could say that,' he replied, trying to make light of the matter.

'I have play fights with Jimmy sometimes. I have to let him win, otherwise he sulks.'

'I see.' But he didn't. He didn't know who Jimmy was. He was about to ask.

'Jimmy's my imaginary friend.'

Gareth looked at her curiously. Had she read his mind, or was it just that she was used to people asking that question?

'You haven't met him,' she continued. 'He's quite shy actually. And Mummy often blames me for things he does, which is annoying. What's your imaginary friend called?'

'Harvey,' Gareth replied, wincing even as he spoke. He did not wish to be reminded of that name, and now he suddenly envisaged Megan constantly asking after him.

'I mean Henry,' he added quickly.

She looked at him curiously, as if wondering how he could be unsure of his imaginary friend's name.

'Henry's nicer than Harvey,' she concluded.

'I agree.'

'Mummy says Auntie Helen's gone away.'

He could not look her in the face. Instead his gaze dropped to the ground.

'That's right,' he replied calmly.

'Is she coming back soon?'

'I don't think so.'

'Where has she gone?'

'She's gone to live with someone else.'

'Oh. So it's a bit like Daddy. Mummy says he went to live with someone else.'

'Oh dear,' said Gareth, shaking his head and looking at her sadly. He had guessed that Megan's father had found someone else. Helen's *someone else* was away at the moment, but he would be coming back. The thought of his return was unbearable. Gareth pictured the occasion, saw her run to greet him, imagined the tightness of the embrace, the passion of their kisses, the hasty ascent to the bedroom. This moment was yet to come, but when it did Gareth felt sure he would somehow know it, that it would cause his body to writhe with agony. The very thought of it sent a wave of pain right through him.

'Are you sick?' Megan enquired softly. He looked up at her again, a little surprised that such a young child could be so perceptive. It was almost as though she could read his thoughts, and share his feelings. He remembered the moment on Friday night when he had heard her crying and then stop apparently at his beckoning, and wondered whether there might exist a mysterious connection between them.

'No, I'm okay,' he answered, but even as he spoke she shook her head. She continued this movement for some seconds, as if to emphasise her disbelief. She was leaning forward, so that her chin was resting on top of the hedge. It appeared to Gareth as though her head was growing out of the dense privet. He watched intently as her face wobbled from side to side. Under different circumstances he might even have found something vaguely humorous in this sight. Was she doing it deliberately, in an attempt to cheer him up? He managed to force a smile, just as her head came to rest.

'What's that book for?' she asked finally.

'It's my journal.'

'What's a journal?'

'It's like a diary.'

'Jimmy keeps a diary. I don't need one, though, because I'm cleverer than him.' She looked round momentarily in the direction of the bathroom window. She wanted to be sure her mother was still in the shower; she might tell her off if she heard what she was about to ask.

'Could I have I look at your diary?'

He hesitated, not wanting to rebuff her, but reluctant to let her see the personal information it contained. Somehow he felt sure that her reading ability would be sufficient for her to understand some of it.

'Oh please, Mr Bell!'

'I'll tell you what; I'll read some of it to you.' He flicked back a few pages, to less significant entries recorded before the start of the school holidays. He came across a passage describing the sports day which he had organised. It had gone well and was likely to be interesting to Megan, whom he knew enjoyed running and jumping. As he began to read he wished that it were as easy to turn the clock back to happier occasions.

Gareth looked up from time to time to check whether he was holding the little girl's attention. He was satisfied that she seemed engrossed in what he was saying. Suddenly, however, he realised that she was no longer there. Sitting up, he noticed her, leaning over the fence at the rear of the property. Gareth got to his feet, just in time to see a large, black dog begin to climb the fence. As Megan started to run, the Dobermann dropped down into the garden.

'Mummy, mummy,' Megan cried as she made for the back door. Gareth hurried towards the hedge. The dog was scampering across the lawn towards his little neighbour.

'Mummy, help!' Megan shouted. Gareth realised the little girl might not make it indoors before the dog got to her. He could hear that the shower was still running in the bathroom above. If Jenny had heard her daughter's call she would surely have come to the window by now. As the Dobermann got close to Megan she stumbled, and fell flat on her face on the stone path. She began to squeal as the dog came and stood over her. Gareth was trying to clamber over the hedge, but the privet was too dense and he found himself sinking into it. He was forced to climb out of the foliage, step back, and take a running jump. One foot caught the top of the hedge on the way down. Gareth landed awkwardly and twisted his right ankle as he fell into the flower-bed. Heedless of the pain, he scrambled to his feet, and hobbled towards the Dobermann. Megan had rolled over onto her back, and was looking up at the dog. Gareth tried to grab its collar, but the Dobermann was too strong and wriggled free. Above the struggle the bathroom window opened. Jenny's squeals began to echo those of her daughter. As Gareth grappled with the Dobermann it suddenly turned on him, sinking its teeth into the same ankle he had injured moments earlier. Megan was quickly on her feet, just as her mother came out into the garden, a hastily donned dressing-gown swirling around her. Megan rushed to her mother and jumped into her arms. Instinctively Jenny lifted her daughter up to her shoulders, and turned towards the cottage. Gareth was still trying to free himself. Clutching a post with both hands, he was able to keep his balance. But he could not loosen the dog's grip on his ankle, and his trouser leg afforded little protection from the animal's sharp incisors. Jenny was heading for the back door. But Megan was looking over her shoulder.

'Mummy, help Mr Bell!' she pleaded. Jenny swung round and looked anxiously back down the garden. Beyond Gareth's pained face was another, peering over the fence from the open field which bordered the rear of the cottage. A spotty lad with dishevelled hair called out: 'Satan, get over here!'

The Dobermann let go of Gareth's leg and looked towards the foot of the garden.

'Come here, git!' The boy's voice was louder this time, and the dog responded. A few moments later it was scrambling back over the fence. The boy turned and began to head back across the field.

'Wait!' cried Gareth. 'You can't just walk away from this!' He tried to run towards the bottom of the garden, but found it was quicker and less painful to hop. He stopped short of the back fence. The boy was jogging, with the dog at his heel, towards the woods at the far end of the field.

'Come back!' yelled Gareth, his anger rendering him oblivious to his throbbing leg. But the boy didn't look back.

As Gareth stood, helplessly watching the guilty pair disappear from view, he became aware that Jenny was just behind him

'All right, boy?' she asked.

Gareth tried not to grimace as he looked down at his ankle.

'Well, I'll live,' he replied, forcing a smile.

'Get 'ee up Dr Ross, quick,' said Jenny. 'I'll take 'ee up in me car. 'Ere, put yer arm over me shoulder.'

Gareth did as Jenny suggested and they made their way back across the lawn towards the cottage.

Chapter 11

It was a relief to finally reach Bodmin, thought Andrew as he drove up the hill approaching the roundabout on the edge of town. He had taken the afternoon off work at short notice, with the intention of spending some time with his brother, about whom he was becoming increasingly concerned. Before setting off he had returned home for lunch, and then walked down to the store to stock up for the weekend. It was a hot Friday afternoon, the second day of August, and Polzeath was inevitably packed with tourists. Even his progress round the store had been slow, and there were several people ahead of him in the queue. Just as he joined the back of it he realised who was standing immediately in front of him. He hesitated over whether to talk to her. For some reason she glanced over her shoulder: perhaps she had caught a whiff of his familiar scent. Their eyes met long enough to confirm recognition before she turned back. For a few seconds he thought she was going to ignore him, but then she turned round again. The look in her eyes foreshadowed her question:

'Do you hate me?'

'I don't hate anybody.'

'How's Gareth?'

'He's, well . . . not so good, to be honest with you, Helen. I'm going to see him this afternoon. Is there anything you want me to pass on to him?'

'No, there's nothing, thanks.'

Helen glanced over her shoulder. The queue had edged forwards, and Helen was next in line.

'Are you going straight home?' she asked.

He nodded.

'I'll wait for you.'

As Andrew came out of the store and into the blazing sunshine, he saw that Helen had crossed the road. She was bending over a bicycle, which had been left leaning against a lamppost.

She smiled as he approached.

'Gareth wanted to buy me a bike for my birthday, only we couldn't find one that I really liked.'

She stood up and took a step backwards.

'One like this would have been just right,' she added wistfully.

As they began to walk back up the slope, Andrew took the opportunity to ask:

'Did you really have to leave, Helen? I mean, you hardly know Harvey. Couldn't you have given it some time before you made up your mind? I don't know how Gareth's ever going to get over this.'

He saw how uncomfortable she looked.

'I know it's going to be difficult for him, but I hope in time he'll find someone else, someone who'll be much, much better for him than I am. It's only duty that's made me stay with Gareth as long as I have. Now I've met Harvey I know what it should feel like. Isn't it better to admit that you made a mistake a long time ago and at least give everyone concerned a chance of happiness?'

Andrew felt unable to protest further. If anything he found her argument persuasive.

'How's Cassie?' she wanted to know.

'I haven't seen her for some time.'

'Oh, I see.'

It was strange that she should have asked. Cassie had called him the previous evening. For a moment, he toyed with the idea of going into detail, but then he thought better of it. He was more interested in gleaning further information from Helen.

'When does Harvey get back?'

'At the beginning of next month.'

'Oh, not until then.'

'Yes, it's a long time.'

Andrew was quick to spot a ray of hope. Was it long enough for a change of heart, he wondered?

'Won't you be lonely on your own?'

'A little, but that's the least of my problems at the moment.'

'Listen, if there's anything you need, call on me, okay?'

'That's really kind of you, particularly under the circumstances.'

She hesitated a moment, before adding:

'Listen, I do care about Gareth, you know.'

Andrew tried not to look too sceptical. What mattered was whether she cared enough to go back to him, he thought. It was better not to point that out, though; it would seem as though he was pressuring her. So he simply nodded his head.

Again she hesitated.

'Andrew, have you ever seen any other women visiting Harvey?'

He pondered for a moment. How he wished he could say yes! But he simply shook his head.

'I'm not at home that much, and when I am I'm too busy to notice things like that.'

She thanked him and left him to his shopping. The thought that Harvey might have someone else lingered in Andrew's mind as he walked back up the hill. On the face of it, it seemed unlikely. It would be taking too much of a risk to encourage Helen to stay at his house. However, she must have discovered something that gave her cause to be suspicious. Andrew resolved to keep his eyes open just in case. From his front room, he could see enough of Harvey's property over the immediate neighbour's garden. There would be a sort of poetic justice if, having been the person who had facilitated the lovers' introduction, he were somehow able to provide the catalyst which led to the end of the affair. As he journeyed across to Bodmin, his progress hampered by the volume of traffic, Andrew considered how a less scrupulous person might behave in the circumstances. It would be so easy to invent suspicious sightings, spread unsubstantiated rumours, and cast unfounded aspersions on Harvey's character - so easy too, to justify such action in the name of putting an end to his brother's ordeal. He half wished that he could be like that, but he knew his sense of decency would not permit it. No, he would just have to hope that Helen had indeed discovered something which would put a stop to the affair and lead her to give her devoted husband a second chance.

As he parked the car Andrew debated whether to mention Helen's intriguing question to his brother. He decided against it, in case he gave Gareth false hope. It would be better to see what, if anything, came to light first.

As Andrew approached the front door of the cottage he noticed that the garden was beginning to show signs of neglect. He waited for Gareth to appear, but there was no response to the sound of the doorbell. Gareth's car was parked in its usual place near the front gate, and Andrew had phoned him the previous evening and told him of his intention to visit him that afternoon. The absence of a response to his loud knock on the door made Andrew feel a little concerned. Remembering he had a spare key, he decided to let himself in. Once inside he called his brother's name. Still there was no reply. He entered the lounge. The curtains were drawn, making the room curiously dark despite the endeavours of the blazing summer sun to penetrate the gloom. Could this be deliberate, Andrew wondered, or was Gareth so caught up in his problems that even basic actions such as drawing back the curtains were being overlooked? Seeing that the kitchen was clearly unoccupied, Andrew returned to the hallway and called up the stairs. Again there was no reply. He decided to try the back garden. Once more he called his brother's name to no avail. But as he moved on down the path he caught sight of a foot protruding from the end of the bench at the bottom of the garden. Then the rest of Gareth's prostrate form came into view. He was lying flat on his back on the bench, with his eyes closed. On the stone path near Gareth's hand was a wine bottle, and as Andrew edged closer he could see that another one had rolled under the seat. For some moments Andrew stood and stared at him, wondering whether it might be better to leave him to his slumbers. Suddenly Gareth opened his eyes and began to sit up straight.

'So how's the ankle now?' Andrew asked.

'Better, thanks, the doctor said I just needed to rest it.'

'And the bite?'

It's healing well, thanks.'

Gareth pulled down his sock to reveal the mark left by the Dobermann's teeth.

'Have you been standing there long?' he asked.

'Long enough to realise what a bad way you're in,' Andrew replied. The tone of his voice was sympathetic; nevertheless Gareth responded as one who had been chastised:

'I must have nodded right off.'

Andrew looked down at the empty bottle standing on the ground.

'Well, you soon polished that off!'

Gareth had to think for a moment.

'No, I started it at lunchtime, and brought it out here to finish up.'

'What did you have for lunch?'

'Oh . . . just some toast.'

'I suppose that goes rather well with a bottle of Chablis?' Andrew's worried look said it all.

'I just needed something to soothe me, so that I could get some sleep.'

Andrew sat down beside his brother.

'Couldn't you take some sleeping tablets?'

'I haven't got any. Don't worry, I won't make a habit of it.'

Andrew reached under the seat and pulled out the other bottle.

'What about this one?'

Gareth looked embarrassed.

'Okay, so I did the same thing yesterday. I'm just doing it to relax. I'll be all right, don't worry.'

'You know, you need to get out and do something, if only to take your mind off things.'

Gareth looked pensive. Normally he spent the early part of the summer holidays in a leisurely manner, walking on the moors, and reading - mainly historical and factual books. He had been content to let Helen organise their social life. The few people he might have had contact with at this time of the year were essentially 'her friends'.

'I'll try to find something to get involved with,' he concluded, but even as he spoke he wondered what he could do in this respect. Using his imagination was not one of his strong points, and the likelihood of finding some activity to distract him from his heartache seemed remote.

'Good', Andrew replied, 'but make it something where you'll make some new friends.'

He paused, aware that Gareth was looking doubtful. Not wanting to stare, Andrew allowed his gaze to drop. A ladybird had found a space on the seat between them and was crawling towards Andrew. He focused on the insect while he struggled to find something to say which would give his brother some form of encouragement. Then he remembered what he had been meaning to tell him:

'I heard from Cassie last night.'

'Really?' Gareth responded. The look on his face said it all. Andrew smiled: he knew that Gareth considered Cassie too unfathomable, and their relationship too unpredictable.

'I said no.'

Gareth looked curiously at his brother, reminding Andrew that he, too, had been surprised by his response. He hadn't quite understood what it was that had given him the strength to finally turn her down. Just at that moment it dawned on Andrew that his refusal was at least in part a declaration of solidarity with his brother. If Gareth was going to go without love, then so would he.

'What did she say?'

'She was upset. She begged me to think about it.'

'And will you?'

'Maybe. It's not high on my list of priorities at the moment.'

Gareth managed a smile, likewise sensing that Andrew's decision was in some way bound up with his own situation, feeling that an expression of gratitude was called for but unable to think how to formulate it. They sat together, still and silent for perhaps a minute, before Gareth continued:

'I wish I could be so blasé about Helen.'

64

'Well, you haven't had time to get used to being without her yet. I've had plenty of chances to adjust to being without Cassie over the years.'

Gareth nodded.

'I still hope she'll come back to me, you know.'

'I know.'

'Do you think there's a chance?'

Andrew pondered for a moment, trying to avoid excessive pessimism on the one hand, and false hope on the other.

'You can never tell for sure with things like this. One thing I would say, though. Let whatever's going to happen with Harvey happen. If you try to intervene, she'll turn against you and then she won't come back even if things go wrong between them.'

Gareth looked down at the path as though contemplating this advice. Seeing how dismayed his brother looked, Andrew sensed the time was right to make his other revelation.

'Actually, I saw Helen earlier on.'

Gareth looked up.

'Where?'

'I bumped into her down at the store.'

Gareth looked disappointed. Andrew guessed that his brother had been hoping he would say that she had come to see him.

'What did she say?'

Andrew hesitated. The most significant thing was the very thing he had decided to keep quiet about for the time being.

'She wanted to know how you were.'

'What did you say?'

'I told her the truth.'

'So she does still care about me.'

Andrew nodded.

'But there's a difference between caring about someone and wanting to be with them as a partner.'

Andrew's remark was met with a look of resignation

'Isn't there any chance you could find someone else eventually?'

Gareth sighed.

'I've asked myself the same question many times already.'

'And?'

'I'm sure I could find someone I was attracted to, and maybe find that they felt the same for me. But could I ever really be with them, knowing that I'm still in love with Helen? You see, when I married Helen, I gave myself completely to her. I meant what I said about forsaking all others - for better for worse, and all that. It really was unconditional love. The fact that she's left me for someone else doesn't change that. The only difference is that my love for her no longer makes me happy.'

Andrew sat quietly for a few moments; then he got to his feet, patting his brother on the shoulder as he did so. Eager to conclude the conversation on a positive note, he observed:

'Well, at least I know all this wine you've been drinking hasn't stopped you from thinking straight.'

Gareth forced a smile and nodded.

Andrew began to make his way back down the garden path.

'I'll make you a coffee,' he called over his shoulder.

Gareth stayed where he was for some moments; then he stood up abruptly, causing a wave of pain to pass through his head. The garden seemed to be rotating slightly. Nevertheless he hurried after his brother, anxious to get to the kitchen ahead of him. He had remembered he had left his journal on the worktop, and if he was not mistaken it was open at the page where the previous day's entry could be found.

Chapter 12

As she lay back down Helen glanced at the digital bedside clock: it was 2:30 a.m. She had drifted off to sleep just before midnight, but soon afterwards a crash of thunder had brought her out of her slumber with a jolt. The storm had only lasted about ten minutes, but it had taken her much longer to get back to sleep. She had attributed the latest disturbance to a nightmare. There had been several that week. Helen understood them as an expression of the deep sense of guilt which was threatening to become her constant shadow. She had begun to wonder whether she should go and confess to a priest; perhaps she would receive some form of reassurance about what God would have to say in the final reckoning. In her darkest dream she saw herself being brought before Him. He was a magistrate-like figure, in a red gown and a wig. She was kneeling down, her head bowed, and He was asking her to account for everything she had done. There would just be the one major crime to report, that of causing sudden devastation to someone who loved her very much, otherwise nothing too drastic. Perhaps she should go back to Gareth. That could be her punishment. But then would she break Harvey's heart instead? No, she assured herself, Harvey was too tough for that, and too taken up with the success he was experiencing with *Kosmos* to allow anyone to bring him down. He would be hurt, but he would get over it and move on to someone else. If anything, *she* might be the one whose heart would get broken. True, there had been no more mysterious calls, and Harvey had denied having any idea who had left the suspicious message. He had promised to listen to it with her when he got back and try to get to the bottom of it. He had even sounded upset at the implication that she didn't entirely trust him. There was no doubt that he had given all the right answers. Yet some instinct was telling her not to be too ready to accept his assurances.

Anxiety about Harvey's integrity was less prominent in her mind than her troubled conscience, yet neither made pleasant bedfellows. As she rolled over onto her front on a mattress which seemed far too large for her alone, she thought she heard a rattling sound coming from the floor below. Normally the silence in the house was oppressive, and she slept with the window open so that she could hear the reassuring sound of the waves breaking on Polzeath beach. Tonight she had been forced to shut the window to keep out the rain which had accompanied the thunder.

Helen was struggling to recall the content of her latest dream, and was no longer convinced that this was what had awoken her. Suddenly a sound from below suggested an alarming alternative. Again she found herself sitting bolt upright, straining to identify the source of the dull thud which had startled her. Once again her heart was racing, thumping audibly, and her breasts were heaving. Another noise - a faint creaking sound, unmistakably that of a door opening, spurred her into action. In an instant she was out of bed, groping for the chair by the wall and the silk nightgown she had strewn across it. Hastily she wrapped the gown around her body. Nervous fingers fumbled to tie a bow in the belt.

The bedroom door was slightly ajar, enabling her to open it silently. She edged closer to the rail which separated the landing from the stairs, until she was just able to peer over the top into the gloom at the bottom of the staircase. She knew that she had left the lounge door closed, and now it was wide open. The flickering light coming from within suggested that whoever was in there was shining a torch. Helen stepped back and took a couple of deep breaths, telling herself not to panic. Her first thought was that it must be a burglar, but then her mind went back to the unexplained message - was someone trying to scare her? A third possibility struck her: could it be Gareth? Had the ordeal she was putting him through affected him so badly that he had gone off the rails?

Another sound from below - a clonking noise, as when one object is knocked against another, gave her a start, and she banged her elbow on a drawer behind her. Somehow she stifled her impulse to yelp, and concentrated her attention on the question of how to deal with her predicament. She could stay where she was, or she could go back into the bedroom and hide: under the bed was a possibility, or there was room in the wardrobe. But if her adversary came upstairs she would be trapped. Even if she hid successfully, how long would she have to hold on before she could be certain that the coast was clear? She contemplated the possibility of escape. There was just one staircase, with the open door to the lounge and its occupant very close to the bottom. She could make a run for it, or she could try to sneak out. At least if she got as far as the front door undetected, she should have enough of a head start to get well clear of the house and into a position to scream for help if the intruder chose to give chase. She risked a look over the railing again. The light from the torch was very dim, and she could hear a noise so faint it seemed to have come from the far end of the lounge. She tiptoed round to the top of the staircase, took another deep breath and, keeping close to the wall, ventured the first step. She took courage from the fact that her bare feet made almost no sound on the thickly carpeted stairs; indeed the rapid thumping of her heart seemed infinitely louder. In no time she found herself at the bottom of the stairs. From there it was perhaps a dozen paces to the front door, but from that point on there was an extra dimension to her terror: her back was now turned to the lounge door. She started to creep through the hallway, but a sudden noise from the lounge caused her to take fright. It was no more than the sound of a creaking floorboard, but it was enough to propel her into a run for the front door. She grabbed the handle and flung it open, but managed to catch it and prevent it from slamming against the wall, leaving her with a glimmer of hope that the intruder might have failed to hear her make her escape. She did not stop to look back and, ignoring the path to the front gate, raced across the grass and scrambled over the front wall. Her gown caught on the jagged edge of a brick and ripped. Helen swore under her breath but kept going. The road at this point was rough and stony, and she hurt her bare feet continually, but nothing was going to impede her from getting away. She ignored the immediate neighbour, whose house was in total darkness. On reaching the gate to Andrew's house she saw that a light was on in an upstairs room. She took a quick look behind her. Mercifully, there was no sign of the intruder. Helen plucked up the nerve to run down the path to Andrew's front door. From here she could just see the entrance to Harvey's house, and if anyone emerged she would at least have some decent hiding places to choose from. She dared to press the bell. Against the silence which surrounded her it sounded agonisingly loud, and she peered anxiously back up the hill.

A sound from above made her step back. A window eased open, and Helen could see the mystified look on Andrew's face.

'Help!' She took another furtive look to her right. 'There's someone in the house.'

Andrew was at the front door in seconds. No sooner had he opened it than Helen tumbled inside. She was beginning to shiver. Instinctively he put his hands on her shoulders and pulled her to him.

'Someone's got inside, in the lounge.'

'Are you sure?'

'Yes, I could hear them moving around.'

'I'll go and take a look.'

'No, call the police.'

'I'll take my mobile with me. We can call them when we've got a better idea what's going on.'

He let her go, turned and retrieved his phone from his jacket.

'It'll take ages for them to get here,' he pointed out. 'The nearest police station is in Wadebridge.'

'We should call them anyway. What's the matter? Don't you believe me? Do you think I'm imagining it?'

'No, it's not that . . .'

'Well then?'

She looked at him suspiciously. Had the same thought that had occurred to her earlier crossed his mind?

'We can call on the way up. I want to see if there's anything I can do. If they're still there, I may try to keep them pinned down until the police arrive.'

He was through the front doorway before she could respond. She followed him down the path, full of admiration at his readiness to intervene. But was he being reckless? She wondered what Harvey would do, given the same situation. She still didn't know him well enough to know the answer to that question. As for Gareth, she felt sure he would have the sense to wait until the police arrived. Andrew was tall and well built, and would be likely to get the upper hand in a fight. But what if the intruder was armed?

'Andrew, don't go doing anything stupid. It's not worth it.'

She was having difficulty keeping up. He was halfway up the track already.

'Andrew!' She tried not to call too loudly, still conscious of the need to avoid alerting the uninvited guest of their presence.

'What if it's Gareth?'

She cringed with embarrassment as she raised the question.

'It can't be,' he said simply. She wondered whether he really was so certain.

Andrew turned, hurried up the hill, and jumped the wall into Harvey's front garden. Helen was able to clamber over more deliberately than when she had made her escape. The front door was slightly ajar. Andrew pushed it open and stepped inside. He was greeted by a gloomy silence. After a few seconds he was able to make out what he assumed must be the lounge door. He was about to move towards it when he remembered that they still hadn't called the police. He turned to see where Helen was. She was not far behind him. Fear of remaining outside on her own had compelled her to follow Andrew almost to the door; but to actually go back inside the house was another matter, and she was on the verge of deciding to leave him to it. After all, he was the one who had insisted on doing this.

Helen was surprised to see Andrew facing towards her, but when he took his mobile and held it out to her she immediately realised what they had overlooked. He pointed down the hill. She turned and hurried back to the road.

There were still no signs of activity inside. Andrew had mixed feelings as he tiptoed quickly down the hallway. He had always had a secret longing to be a hero, to risk his life to protect someone else, to know that there had been a moment when his courage had been put to the test and not been found wanting. Here was such an occasion, and he had made it as far as the very brink of danger without the slightest hint of hesitation. Now, however, as he stopped inches short of the lounge door, he prepared himself for the bottom line. The same possibility that had occurred to Helen suddenly struck fear into him.

He squinted in the darkness for some means of defending himself, but there was nothing, He could go back for some sort of tool. But if he returned to an empty room he would never know whether the time spent doing this had made the difference between success and failure. Andrew summoned up the nerve to press on. He tried once more to pick up some clue as to his quarry's whereabouts, but he could hear no sound from within the lounge. In a bid to calm his nerves he took a deep breath, then span round into the doorway. The room was darker than the hallway, and for a few seconds he was forced to wait for his eyes to adjust. Finally some of the larger objects began to take shape: a chest of drawers, a couple of armchairs, and a table. All appeared immobile. Andrew took an uneasy step forward into the room. He could make out the window that overlooked the back garden. The curtain was drawn back on one side, and the part of the window behind it was open. Had the intruder made his getaway, or was this just the means of entry? Could he be hiding in this room, or perhaps elsewhere in the house? Andrew decided to risk putting the light on. He felt around on the wall beside him, anxious not to turn his back on the scene, in case this gave his foe the opportunity to spring from his hiding place. When at last his trembling fingers did manage to locate something, he was not even sure it was a light switch. There was a knob in the middle He tried pushing to no effect, then realised it was a dimmer switch. He turned it, and slowly the light came on. Finally Andrew was able to take a proper look around him.

Chapter 13

'The daytimes are difficult enough, Joey, but the nights are something else.' The budgie looked up at his owner suspiciously, his head tilted at an odd angle. Gareth had done away with the routine of covering the cage at night. Although some aspects of the rituals observed before Helen left had simply been neglected, leaving the bird visible was a deliberate decision, because Joey at least embodied some sort of companion. The television was a distraction, but communication was all one way. With the budgie, some form of interaction was possible. For a start, Joey would move around the cage in a way which relieved the room from being totally stagnant. And although his chirps were meaningless to Gareth, they were pleasant enough as a form of background noise. Sometimes Joey would nuzzle up to the toy bird which shared his perch and chortle in a way which Gareth found quite soothing. Above all, Joey was a good listener. It was easy to get his attention, he didn't interrupt, and you could bare your soul to him. And there was no need at all to be careful about what you said, or to worry about offending him.

'Do you know what the time is, Joey? Eh? Half past one in the morning. I was actually in bed, just starting to doze, and this bloody thunderstorm comes along. Did it frighten you, eh? What do you reckon your mistress is doing? Fast asleep without a care in the world, no doubt. Whereas you and I, we are the watchmen of the night. Yes, that's right young bird. So what shall we do, eh? We could play a game, or I could take you for a walk. Would you like that?'

The budgie chose that moment to ruffle his feathers, before resuming his curious pose. Gareth's train of thought was interrupted for a moment. He reached out a hand to steady the cage - for it, like the rest of the room, was spinning.

'Or we could go for a drive! How about that? No, we can't do that, I've had too much wine, you know, it wouldn't be legal. I know, I'll read to you. Then we'll sober up, and then we'll go out for a while. How about that? Any objections? No? Okay! Listen carefully! I'm going to ask you questions afterwards.'

Gareth let go of the cage so that he had both hands free to hold up the journal. It was open at the page which contained the entry he had made earlier that evening, shortly after Andrew had gone home.

'*Friday the second of August,*' he announced. '*Phew! Andrew nearly saw what I wrote yesterday. Managed to whisk it out from under his nose. Can't have him being any more worried than he is already. He insisted he would come over on Sunday. I'm grateful, of course, although actually I don't feel like seeing anyone, not even him. 10.15 pm marked the moment exactly one week ago when she left. No word from her since then, just that one painful encounter on Monday morning. Did as requested and kept out of the way when she came in this morning. Spent some time looking to see what she had taken. Had to spray air freshener to take away that scent.*'

Gareth looked up. He nodded his approval at the bird.

'Glad to see you're still following closely, little friend.'

He scanned the rest of the page.

'Want to hear some more?' He turned back a page. 'Ah, yes, now you'll like this bit. You get a mention.'

The bird began to chirrup.

'*Wednesday the thirty-first. Spent some time in the garden, talking to Megan. She wanted to know who it was she had heard me talking to. I explained that it must have been Joey.*'

Gareth paused and grinned at the bird. 'I told you I gave you a mention,' he added. 'Now where was I? Oh yes! *She seemed worried. Apparently chatting to imaginary friends is quite normal, whereas talking to pets isn't.*'

Gareth looked up again. 'What do you think, Joey? Don't lots of people have conversations with their budgies? *She* never used to talk to you, I know. But why should that stop me?'

He scanned the lines which followed the point at which he had stopped. The budgie was still chattering merrily.

'Sorry, young bird, I forgot I was supposed to be reading to you. This is fascinating stuff, don't you think? Listen, what do you make of this? *I told Megan I had heard her crying in the night, and that I was concerned*

74

about her. She said she was missing Jimmy. That's her imaginary friend, you know. *I asked her where Jimmy was. She said she didn't know, only that he had been captured by "the wazzock". She looked very distressed at the mention of this word. I wanted to know more about this creature. The wazzock, she said, was an evil being who has the power to take people away from where they belong, and you may never, ever see them again. She didn't know what the wazzock looked like, only that he lives by the sea.'*

Gareth looked intensely at Joey, who had gone quiet again.

'Tell me, Jo, what do you reckon? Is it just coincidence? Or is Harvey the wazzock? It's a great name for someone who takes your wife away from you! But listen, this is the best bit. *Megan wanted to know if I was scared of the wazzock. I told her there was no such creature. She looked at me as though she didn't believe me. Then she told me I obviously was scared of the wazzock, which was why I wanted to pretend he didn't exist. I assured her I really wasn't scared. So she said to me that I should prove it, that I should go and find the wazzock and challenge him to a fight, and bring Jimmy back to her.*

Is that nonsense, Joey? Is it? Or is there some sort of message in her words. Should I track down Harvey, and challenge him to a fight? Would Helen be impressed? Would it show her a side of me she's never seen before, eh? Would it show her that I'm more of a man than she thinks? And what if Harvey chickened out? What if he wasn't up to a fight? She would hardly be impressed by that, would she? Maybe that would bring her back to me.'

Gareth found himself clenching his fist in readiness for action. Joey seemed to be looking a little nervously at him.

'What do you think, Jo? Should I go after him? Should I?'

Gareth stared down at the bird for several seconds, begging him for some sort of response, but Joey continued to look curiously at him. It occurred to Gareth that here was an occasion when a pet was not much use as a companion - when you actually needed some guidance. People were fallible in that respect, but at least they would usually make some sort of contribution. Gareth turned towards the front window and the uninviting darkness beyond the rain-spattered panes of glass. He snapped the journal shut, startling Joey, who fluttered around the cage before resuming his

75

position on the perch. Gareth sighed. He didn't need the budgie - or anyone else for that matter - to provide an answer to his question. In reality, he knew already: he wasn't going to set out to confront or provoke Harvey. It wasn't that he was afraid of the man; it simply wasn't his way of handling things.

'Sorry Joey, we won't be going out after all.' Gareth gestured in the direction of the front garden. 'Rain stopped play for today,' he concluded. Then he turned, wobbled across to the sofa, fell forwards onto it and buried his face in a cushion.

Chapter 14

It took Helen some seconds to make sense of her surroundings. The room was totally unfamiliar. The wallpaper was not the delicate shade of green that she had come to know over the past week, but was cream coloured, and there was no digital clock staring her in the face as she opened her eyes. The mattress felt harder, and the bed was smaller. It was only when she sat upright that she realised where she was and how she had come to be there.

A pleasant coffee-flavoured aroma was wafting its way in through the door, which had been left slightly ajar. Helen could hear the occasional clanking of crockery. She had no means of knowing the time, but her stomach told her it must be nearer to lunch than breakfast. She got up and went across to the door. She was still wearing the same gown, and she could see now that the tear in it was worse than it had seemed at the time. The sight of it removed any doubt that her memories of the night's events were real. The gown was ruined, but it would do to go downstairs in: the gash stopped just short of her thigh. On the landing she paused and looked in through the open door to Andrew's bedroom. The bed was neatly made, and the room was uncluttered. He had always been more domesticated than his brother, she reflected.

Helen found the kitchen empty. She could see that Andrew was now standing in the back garden, and was talking to the old lady who lived in the house between Harvey's and his own. Presumably he was putting her in the picture as to what had happened. Noticing that a coffee pot and a cup had been left in readiness for her, Helen took a seat and began to pour. It was sweet of Andrew to remember that she always took a large cup in the mornings, she thought. Under the circumstances, Andrew's thoughtfulness was more than she could have asked for. If only she could repay him with some good news . . .

Her mind strayed back to the list of items which had been stolen. Most notable were the expensive stereo system which Harvey had bought shortly after he had moved in, the camcorder and the video player. The karaoke machine was also missing, although the small portable TV which went with it had turned up in the back garden. The main TV had been spared, presumably because it was too large to carry, and the home computer and its accessories had escaped because the burglar had left the study untouched. Helen had watched from the safety of Andrew's front garden as first the lounge light came on, then one by one the other downstairs lights, and finally the upstairs lights. Andrew's reappearance in Harvey's doorway coincided with the arrival of the police, and Helen had looked on while the officers examined the premises.

There had been no sign of the intruder, who had left via the back garden immediately after Helen had made her getaway. Helen was relieved to learn that there was no reason to think that Gareth had been involved. A broken window in a downstairs toilet indicated the means of entry. The police were of the opinion that the intruder had passed the loot through the lounge window to an accomplice, who had ferried the items up the path to a getaway vehicle. It had taken some time to establish exactly what had been taken, and by the time the police had left daybreak was barely an hour away. Nevertheless Helen had been uncomfortable about the prospect of remaining alone in the house for the rest of the night, and had gratefully accepted Andrew's offer to let her stay in his spare room.

Some minutes passed before Andrew finished explaining to the neighbour and came back into the kitchen. Helen was just taking the last sip of her coffee.

'Sorry about that,' he began'. 'Mrs Parfitt wanted to know all the details.' He noticed the empty cup. 'Would you like some more?'

'No, thanks.'

'How about some breakfast?'

'No, thanks all the same. I had better get back home.'

She pulled a face as she finished the sentence, embarrassed at the admission that she now thought of Harvey's house as home.

Andrew pretended not to notice.

'I was just about to have a fry-up. Are you sure you won't join me? You must be hungry by now.'

'What time is it?'

'It's nearly midday.'

She could see how concerned he looked, and felt obliged to change her mind.

'Okay, but I'll have to go straight afterwards. I want to get the place back together as soon as possible.'

In truth, she was anxious to check her mobile phone, which she had left behind in the bedroom. Harvey had promised to send her a text that morning.

'Will you be all right, up there on your own?' Andrew enquired.

'Oh, I'll cope,' she assured him. 'It won't be easy, I know, but I'll have to put it behind me.'

Andrew began to gather the ingredients for the fry-up. It had crossed his mind that if Helen was having second thoughts about her decision, then the events of that night might sway her further in the direction of returning to Gareth. He wondered whether Helen had read his mind: her answer had been unequivocal, putting an end to any fresh hope that might have arisen. He concluded that she must indeed have followed his train of thought. She really was quite a shrewd woman, he thought, as he tipped oil in the pan. He turned towards her, intending to check whether there was anything she wouldn't eat. She had poured another coffee and was stirring it intently. Andrew refrained from asking about the meal, and took the opportunity to have a good look at her. He had never thought of her as an attractive woman. Perhaps the abundance of ginger hair was something which appealed greatly to some men, and not at all to others. He could see that she was too lost in thought to be aware that he was staring at her, and this enabled him to contemplate her at his leisure. What was it about her that made her seem different all of a sudden? There were several possibilities. Until yesterday's encounter in the shop he had only ever seen her when she was with Gareth. He had no idea what she was like when she was away from him. Nor had he ever seen her in a state of undress before. Now here she was with just a flimsy, silk nightgown on, sitting totally at ease in his kitchen. That was something Cassie would never have done. Even after all the years they had known each other, she would have insisted on being fully dressed before going downstairs for breakfast; this was a side of her character he had always found frustrating. Andrew's mind went back to the moment in the middle of the night when he had drawn Helen to him, and held her against him. He had had no motive other than to console her, yet he was concerned that he had found the few seconds during which they had been close pleasurable. For the first time he had noticed how enticing her smell was, and now he was faintly aware of it again. He saw that her normally pale skin had turned to a golden colour as the summer had progressed, and her cheeks appeared rosier than he remembered, in a way which made her seem warmer. He couldn't help feeling irritated: he didn't even want to *think* of her as attractive, let alone discover that he was actually turned on by her.

It was not just that she was his brother's wife, and therefore strictly out of bounds; it was the treacherous streak in her which made him want to see her as someone undesirable. Yet he had felt drawn to her when she had turned up, frightened and vulnerable on his doorstep. And now, suddenly, he found himself forced to admit that she could be pleasing to look at.

He noticed her raise her eyes without lifting her head, and realised that she had sensed he was watching her. She looked up, tossed her head back and smiled reassuringly. It seemed to him that she was used to being noticed. It was as though she took it for granted that men would be drawn to her. It crossed his mind to ask her whether she had ever experienced rejection. Instead, he merely returned to the question of what she would like for breakfast.

As he watched while the bacon and eggs started to sizzle, Andrew carried on pondering why Helen seemed different, and came to a conclusion about the main factor: Harvey's influence. Helen had been struggling for a long time to fulfil the role that all around her had made her feel it was her duty to perform, that of the loyal wife of a steady, respectable man. Andrew knew something about Harvey from an interview he had heard on the radio shortly after he had become his neighbour. By his own admission Harvey was unconventional: he set his own objectives in life and as long as these were met he was satisfied. He claimed not to care what anyone thought of him, and that he was far more interested in what people thought of his music, and whether it would still be played long after he was gone. He refused to take any credit for his compositions, insisting that he was simply a vehicle through which a mysterious creative force passed.

Andrew had listened intently to the interview and had concluded that Harvey was quite a fascinating character. And if this was the impression

Harvey left on another man, then it was hard to imagine how deep his impact on women must be, particularly in view of his obvious good looks. Andrew could see quite clearly now that it was Helen's relationship with Harvey which had changed her. It was as though she had been set free from a trap, empowered to be her true self, granted the freedom to indulge herself in a way she had only ever dreamed about beforehand.

The meal that he had cooked in thoughtful silence was ready now. He brought it over to her and she looked warmly at him as she thanked him. She ate with the relish of one who had gone without for some time, causing him to wonder whether the fear she had experienced during the night had somehow affected her appetite. Keeping the conversation to a minimum, he watched her closely as she tucked into the sausages, mushrooms and tomatoes, hoping to take the opportunity to check his perceptions at close range. He found himself wondering about the nightgown, which seemed to suit her so perfectly. Was it a present from Gareth, had she bought it herself, or was it Harvey who had given it to her?

She was just finishing her meal. As she placed her cutlery neatly on her empty plate, she looked up suddenly:

'Penny for your thoughts.' She was smiling again, causing him to feel emboldened.

'I was just thinking what a lovely gown that is.'

'Thank you. It's just a shame it's been ruined.'

'How come?'

She stood up, and turned sideways on to him. He wished she hadn't done that.

'I only bought it a couple of weeks ago' she went on. 'I had to go all the way to Truro. There's just nowhere closer.'

He nodded, and offered her more food. She agreed with feigned reluctance.

As Andrew stood over the frying pan he considered the implications of her reply. 'A couple of weeks ago' meant before she moved out, but after she had begun her affair. The garment had not been bought by Harvey,

81

but had surely been bought for his benefit. And she had travelled some thirty miles in order to find something suitable. She would never have done that for Gareth. And the result was so enticing that even someone who had previously thought her unattractive now found it difficult to take his eyes off her. He couldn't help wanting to convince himself it wasn't true. He glanced again in her direction. She chose this moment to examine one of her fingernails, and for an instant he was able to think of her as ordinary again. His focus returned to his cooking.

It was only when he had emptied the contents of the frying pan onto her plate and turned towards the table that he was confronted with the final confirmation that it wasn't just his imagination, that here was a different Helen, a newly emancipated woman who had taken a course from which it seemed unlikely she would deviate.

She was leaning back on her chair, so that only its rear legs were touching the floor. She allowed her head to tumble backwards until she was looking up at the ceiling. She took a deep breath, and as she did so her gown struggled to contain her breasts, and what had begun as mild cleavage opened up to form a crevice which extended almost to her belly button. She stretched out her arms behind her in the form of an arc until she was able to clasp her hands together. Then as she breathed out she emitted a soft, plaintive groan.

Chapter 15

Gareth opened the journal and entered the date: Monday 5th August. It had been a hot day, and he had stayed in the garden until around nine o'clock, enabling him to become aware for the first time of the extent to which the nights were beginning to draw in. He found himself contemplating the possibility of spending a long, dreary winter alone in the cottage, and could not help shuddering at the thought. Normally around this point in the summer holiday his mind would begin to focus on the new term, which would start in around four weeks' time, but now he felt no enthusiasm for the prospect. In fact on the few occasions he had allowed thoughts of the new academic year to enter his head it was with a large degree of foreboding, as he wondered how he might bring himself to concentrate on the tasks in hand instead of his private ordeal. It was as well that the heartache had not begun during term time, he reflected. Could he really have carried on trying to teach under the circumstances? The deputy head had struggled on when his marriage had broken up a few years before, but Gareth remembered him saying that the marriage had not been working for some time, and that the end had actually come as something of a relief. Now, ten days after Helen had left, Gareth was still in shock, still trying to come to terms with the hurt, the resentment, and the sense of deprivation. Today a new dimension had been added to his solitude, and he was about to record his feelings about it. But first he wanted to look back over the entry for the previous day, written soon after receiving the visit which Andrew had promised when he found him drunk on Friday. He was still trying to make sense of everything his brother had told him.

Gareth skipped the details of the burglary. There was nothing puzzling about these. It was the aftermath he wanted to understand. He found the passage in which he had recorded his conclusions:

I told Andrew not to worry about it, and that he had done the right thing to help Helen in the way that he had, also that I was sure he was mistaken if he thought that her behaviour had anything to do with him. But as for why she left in a hurry as soon as she had finished eating, I don't know. And why did she call later to apologise? Why didn't she make it clear what she was apologising for? And as for thinking it might have been me that broke into the house, I can't believe she would think I might do that.

Andrew's right, Helen has changed. Who knows what she will do now? Is there a chance that the burglary has upset her enough that she won't be able to stay there? And if not, will she come back here? And what if she did? Would there be a chance things would work out for us?

Gareth resumed his deliberations, and spent some minutes lost in thought without having anything to show for it. With a sigh he abandoned this activity in favour of his daily update. Before beginning, he glanced wistfully in the direction of the now empty space in the corner of the room.

I couldn't believe my eyes this morning. I know Joey was supposed to be her pet, but how could she just take him? It's so unfair. I guess she's feeling lonely too, but it was her decision to have an affair, her actions which led to this situation, and Joey was my companion. I expect if I make an issue out of it she will just be dismissive and scornful, and it will just lead to a pointless row. But if I don't object she will think she has the right to take whatever she wants.

It's even quieter here now without him. It's hard to believe a little budgie could make such a difference. I hope she looks after him and remembers to feed him. I don't think she took any birdseed with her.

The reference to feeding set Gareth's mind on a different course. He had eaten very little in the days since Helen's departure. He had never taken much pleasure in eating, still less in preparing food. Helen loved eating out, and was a reasonable cook, and he had been content to leave it to her to choose and prepare their meals, leaving him to clear things away afterwards. Without his wife or even his normal appetite to prompt him, Gareth had got out of the habit of having proper meals, preferring to make do with biscuits, crisps and the occasional slice of toast. He had found that his liquid intake - tea, coffee, and water as well as wine - was sufficient to stave off any promptings of hunger. Andrew had expressed his concern on Friday that Gareth looked as though he had lost weight, and had offered to cook a roast dinner when he came over on Sunday. Gareth had declined the offer, saying that it was just a phase he was going through. Andrew had reiterated his concerns about the extent of his drinking. In order to reassure him, Gareth had abstained while Andrew was there, leaving his brother to finish off a bottle of Jacob's Creek which was left over from the day before. Andrew had stayed the whole afternoon, and it was then that he had put Gareth in the picture as to the events of Friday night and Saturday. At Andrew's suggestion they had walked down towards the town, past the prison, and onto the moors. They discussed carrying on all the way to Helland, but Gareth had to admit he didn't feel up to it. He had difficulty keeping up with his brother on the way back, and it was this outing which made him realise how weak he had become. Andrew had brought with him some vegetables, and together they had made omelettes to go with these. Andrew had eaten with relish, while Gareth, despite his fatigue, had struggled. Although he did manage to end up with a clean plate, he could see that his brother was more concerned than before, and Andrew's parting comment that evening was an appeal to him to eat more healthily.

Gareth had begun the day with the intention of following his brother's advice, but the discovery that Helen had taken Joey, together with his attempts to get to the bottom of her conduct following the burglary, had distracted him from this purpose. When he had gone out into the back garden early in the afternoon, Megan had spotted him and had bombarded him with questions which her mother had evidently been unable to answer, and which tested his understanding of things. He knew that it was the earth which went round the sun, and not the other way round, but where did the moon fit into this system? He was embarrassed to admit that he couldn't help her. Gareth wondered whether Harvey would have known the answer to that question. He had got into the habit of making theoretical comparisons of his own abilities with those of his rival, and it was proving a demoralising experience. On top of the things he had already learned from Helen about Harvey's ambition and his prowess as a lover, Gareth couldn't help feeling there were other ways in which he could not compete. Harvey's lifestyle must surely be more exciting: tours, interviews on the radio, guest appearances on TV shows, a house overlooking the sea, and no doubt a flash car as well. And Harvey had the ability to sing and write songs, whereas Gareth lacked any musical talent. Indeed, when he was a young boy his parents had deterred him from singing, claiming that he was out of tune, and he had never regained the necessary confidence. Even joining in with hymns at weddings and funerals was a daunting task for him, and where possible he would position himself so that nobody would notice if he avoided it altogether.

Then there was the question of humour. Gareth enjoyed watching comedy, but he had never thought of himself as someone who was particularly gifted at amusing people. By contrast he recalled that there

85

was considerable mirth coming from Harvey's direction at the barbecue. He certainly remembered hearing Helen laughing on several occasions. At the time he had simply felt pleased that she was enjoying herself. How foolish he felt, now that he knew the whole truth! Somehow he was sure that Harvey would have been able to enlighten little Megan, and would probably have been able to enrich his answer with some entertaining anecdote.

Until the last few days Gareth had had no idea that he would ever come to feel so inadequate, let alone that it was possible that this would have such a traumatic effect on him. Now as he sat alone amid the gathering gloom his reflections prompted a sense of despondency which was becoming all too familiar. He had discovered that unhappiness could settle upon you like an illness, that a pain which affected your soul could be far worse than an aching head. Sadness could be so far-reaching as to make even the smallest motion an effort; it could impair your bodily functions so that even taking a breath could be such a struggle it could make you gasp; it could so overwhelm you that it became difficult to focus your mind on anything other than your ordeal.

At length Gareth's mind returned to the passage he had considered necessary to hide from his brother. The entry had been made on the Thursday of the previous week, the first day of August:

Yesterday I woke up with a big hangover, and spent the morning in bed, and the afternoon in the garden. For once there was no sign of Megan. By around six o'clock I had completely recovered, and was feeling restless. I had nothing better to do, so I went out for a drive. I had no particular destination in mind. I wanted a change of scenery, so I just drove aimlessly out of Bodmin and onto the A30. Soon I found myself in Launceston. From there I made my way across country towards Bude. I drove north along the A39 for a little while, but then on a whim I did a U-turn at a roundabout and started to head back in this direction. I saw a signpost for Widemouth Bay and decided to go over there. I've never been over that way before. I thought I would stretch my legs, so I parked down by the beach and walked back up and along the cliff top. I have always been afraid of going too near the edge, but this time I plucked up the nerve to find a steep part and stand right above it. I didn't feel at all scared. I closed my eyes and stood there, listening to the sound of the waves braking below, and the gulls squawking. I thought how marvellous it would be to fly, if only once, for just a few seconds. And I thought, if someone came up from behind and pushed me, there and then, I wouldn't be able to stop it. It would happen, I would find out what it was like to sail through the air, and then there would be an end to all this grief. And I prayed, for the first time in a long while I actually prayed, that this might really happen. I stayed there for quite a while, until I heard someone approaching from further up the slope, and I stood still and waited until they passed by. I found I was actually disappointed that they didn't come up to me and push. When I got back to the car I felt really low, and I couldn't even think which way to turn out of the car park. At first I headed back towards Bude, but then I realised it would be quicker to go on past Widemouth Bay, and cut back to the A39 further down the coast. So I turned round. As I came back over the brow of the hill and started to drive back down towards the bay, I looked across to the right. I could see the point where I had been standing minutes beforehand, the place where I was just a step away from oblivion, and I noticed something about the land between the road and the edge of the cliff. It was a bit like a ski slope. A vehicle travelling at speed which left the road just after the brow would miss the steepest part of the slope and end up in the dip short of the cliff face. But one which came over the brow slowly, then turned sharp right, would head straight down the steepest part. It would then have enough momentum to sail over the cliff top, and it would fly through the air for some seconds before it landed in the water below. I tried to put the image behind me, but it stayed with me all the way home. I can see it now, even as I write. I can even feel this place close by me, as though I am destined to take this ride. And I keep asking myself who would miss me if I did? Certainly not Helen. Sure, she might be upset for a while, and no doubt she would feel guilty about it, but it wouldn't actually matter to her that I wasn't there any more. No, the only person who would really care about it is Andrew. He would be devastated. I can still see his face when I broke the news about Mum and Dad. I just couldn't put him through that again. And there would be nobody left for him. He is my only reason for staying in this world. I have resolved that no matter how painful it is -even if it never gets any better - I will have to live with it. I thought of the saying, 'Greater love has no man than this, that he lays down his life for his brother' (or perhaps it's his friend –it doesn't matter), and it dawned on me that it might require even greater love to stay alive against your will for the sake of your brother.

As Gareth finished reading he noticed that his trembling fingers had an unsteady grasp on the journal. He allowed the book to tumble through his hands and between his knees. It shut as it hit the floor. He could feel a shiver running up his back, and was forced to admit that he was beginning to feel really afraid of what was happening to him. He tried to remember everything his father had told him about self-discipline. In particular he recalled the letter he had sent him when he was working abroad and learned that Gareth had been bullied at school: 'Whatever happens to you, however bad things get, always stay dignified. If you can keep your dignity, you will always be able to master adversity, and life will hold no terrors for you.' Gareth had often wondered whether his father had been able to maintain his dignity when he realised Uncle Les was going to crash the plane, and whether this had enabled him to overcome his terror. In recent years Gareth's life had been largely uneventful and he had rarely had reason to feel any fear; on the contrary, everything had gone so smoothly that he had been lulled into a false sense of security. Now, just ten days after the onset of this ordeal, he found himself being overwhelmed by a sickening sensation of panic, as his heart raced at twice its normal pace. He realised that the room was almost in darkness now. Like a frightened child waking after a nightmare, he groped at the table lamp until he found the switch. This seemed to do the trick. The fear began to subside at once. Retaking his seat on the sofa, he found that his hand alighted on the remote control, and he flicked the button which brought life to the television. After a few minutes he was calm enough to retrieve the journal and continue the update.

Had to resort to putting on the television: it was a poor substitute for Joey. Budgies may not be the cleverest of creatures, but at least they're not able to deceive you. Although in some ways I knew Helen very well, in others she was a complete stranger. She turned out to be capable of doing something I would never have believed she could do. I realise now that in any relationship it's not what you know about the other person that counts, it's what you don't know. It will be no use to me now, for I have nothing left to give, and anyway I don't think I would ever be able to trust a woman again. But perhaps that observation will one day be useful to someone else.

Finally found the courage to re-read Thursday's entry. I wish I could say I didn't mean it, and that it was just a reflection of how gloomy I felt at the time. But the truth is I did mean it. I really did hope that someone would come up behind me and push. Am I mad, that I find the prospect of dying less frightening than that of living? And why can I still see that slope? I have to keep reminding myself that it can't be. I must not let my brother down.

Gareth could feel the fear returning. He broke off abruptly and snapped the journal shut. He got to his feet and switched off the television, pausing to look forlornly at the empty corner before extinguishing the light.

Moments later he was trudging up the stairs. At least he was actually going to bed this evening, rather than nodding off on the sofa and then staggering off to bed in the middle of the night, only to sleep erratically until midday or later. Suddenly the silence in the cottage was punctuated by a shrill sound from outside. It caused Gareth such a start that he almost lost his balance, and clutched at the banister in order not to fall back down the stairs. Then he breathed a sigh of relief as he recognised the sound. He turned and went back down to the lounge, and peered through the window. The noise was irritating him now; indeed the continuous repetition of two notes a semitone apart seemed to be mocking him, calling out a name which would remind him of the latest instalment in his tale of woe. He was glad when the door to the other half of the cottage opened and Megan's mother scurried down the path, her car keys poised for action. 'Come on, Jenny, hurry up,' Gareth muttered to himself. Seconds later the noise came to an end. Gareth watched as she came back down the path. Jenny looked in his direction. She must have seen him because she held her hand aloft and seemed to smile apologetically. He nodded, allowed the curtain to fall back into place, and headed once more for the bedroom. As he reached the point where he had almost fallen he realised he could still hear the sound of the alarm echoing in his head. And it still seemed to be calling the same name: 'Joey, Joey, Joey, Joey, Joey, Joey, Joey . . . '

Chapter 16

The sunlight which had roused Helen from her slumbers disappeared in an instant as the first of the clouds moved into a position to spoil the holidaymakers' idyll. Helen had surfaced for long enough that Wednesday morning to ring her office from the mobile phone she had left on the bedside table. The text message for which it had sat in readiness was long overdue. On Monday she had struggled into work, to find that she was unable to prevent her colleagues from noticing her mood. On Tuesday she had used an upset stomach as her excuse for staying at home, and had assured her boss that she fully expected to have recovered in time for a return to work the following day. Although she had gone to bed early on Tuesday evening she had spent most of the night worrying. Occasional background noises provided uncomfortable reminders of the weekend before. Sleep had had to wait until daybreak, and the next thing she knew it was five to nine, the very time she was usually arriving at her desk. So the stomach complaint was used as an excuse again, except that now it was said to have worsened; indeed the thought that it might be food poisoning had crossed her mind. And yes, if she still felt the same later in the day she would book an appointment with the doctor. She promised to keep them posted.

Now it was gone eleven o'clock. Helen looked disbelievingly at the clock on the bedside table. It was so out of character for her to let anything get to her this badly. She reached out and retrieved her mobile phone. Still there was nothing fresh. Maybe it would be worth one more try; after all there might yet be a genuine explanation for the absence of any contact from him. She shook her head, and turned over onto her side, hoping to console herself in yet more sleep. Perhaps she should accept defeat, she reasoned. However busy he might have been, however difficult the tour might be proving, he could have found a few moments in which to send her a text. Indeed, if he cared at all about her or about their relationship he surely would have done so. What was he playing at, though, asking her to live here, unless he had intended to take up where they had left off once he returned? With a sigh Helen began to formulate another message: *'Darling, where are you? Are you okay? I'm getting really worried. Text back a s a p. Your Helen'.*

She hesitated before pressing the 'Send' key. She had sent at least one text each day since the one due on Saturday had failed to arrive. She had tried calling him, but each time she had found that the phone was switched off. At first she had reasoned that if he had been so upset by something that he wanted solitude then he might not thank her for persistently sending texts. Then she concluded that adopting that attitude simply wasn't good enough. She was not prepared to let him treat her like that and she would have to put a stop to it now, before it became a habit.

As Helen pressed the key she checked the screen for an acknowledgment that her message had been sent. Replacing the mobile phone on the bedside table, she waited for the familiar beeps which indicated that a reply had been received.

A few minutes later she gave up, and turned her attention to the question of what she was going to do if it really was all over with Harvey. Could she possibly go back to Gareth? Would he want her back after what she had done? She still hadn't contacted him since the occasion the previous week when he had confronted her with his unfounded suspicions about Rowena and Jarrod's visit. Helen had now come to feel guilty about her reaction. After all, she had been keeping her affair secret from him: it was only natural that he should be feeling confused and distrustful. She had made up her mind to apologise to Gareth, but her preoccupation with Harvey's silence had prevented her from giving much thought to exactly what to say to him. It was hardly the ideal platform on which to attempt to discuss the possibility of a return to the cottage, even if she decided this was the best option. She considered the alternatives. Her parents would probably be glad to have her back, but she would have to leave Peterson's and find another job nearby. And could she live with them? She hated the thought of the foul aroma which hung around after her father smoked a cigar, and the way her mother would insist on knowing where she was going every time she went out. And then there was what they would say about her leaving Gareth. No, she concluded, that had to be a last resort. Her friend Julie would be willing to accommodate her for a short while, but she would have to sleep on the sofa bed in the lounge. In reality, although they were the best of friends, Helen was doubtful that they could live harmoniously for long in such a cramped environment, particularly given Julie's erratic love life. The only other possibility was Andrew. This was the most appealing – he was kind, even-tempered, and a good cook, and his house had plenty of room, but could she bring herself to ask him? He might see it as a means of encouraging her to go back to Gareth, and take her in for that reason. But if she found that she was unable to do this, it would become difficult for her to stay there. And then there was the incident in his kitchen Saturday lunchtime . . .

Helen realised she could hear music: a digital version of *'There's no place like home'* was coming from below. It occurred to her that this was the first time since she had moved in that anyone had rung the doorbell; she didn't know that it played tunes. Helen slipped her dressing gown on and moved swiftly to the front window. She pulled the curtain back slightly so that she could see who it was. The arc of the porch surrounding the front door restricted her view, and at first all she could see were the feet: a man's shoes, large, shiny and stylish, and the bottom of some smart grey trousers. Her heart missed a beat: could it be Harvey? But why would he ring his own doorbell? Perhaps he didn't want to let himself in and scare her. Mindful of the events of the previous Friday, Helen was wary of going to answer the door. A different melody started up. Given time she would have recognised it as the theme tune to the 'Lone Ranger', but in the excitement of the moment its identity was lost on her. It seemed the caller had reason to think that someone was at home. She opened the window, and cried: 'Who is it?' The man took a step backwards and came into view. Her face fell when she realised it wasn't Harvey. She was surprised to see that he was a black man, for there were not many non-white people in Cornwall. Her impression that he was a flamboyant dresser was confirmed now that she could see the rest of him: he was wearing a jacket which matched the trousers, a colourful bow tie, and a grey cap which he raised as he greeted her:

'My name's Courtney, ma'am.'

The name sounded familiar. She studied him for a moment. He looked about sixty, and he had a broad, cheeky smile, which looked like a permanent fixture. Somehow she knew he must be a musician.

'I'm looking for Helen,' he said brightly. 'Is that you, lady?'

She nodded. 'I'll let you in.'

Without stopping to put her slippers on, she tied a knot in the ribbon of her gown, hurried down the stairs and pulled back the bolt on the front door.

'Come in,' she urged.

He wiped his feet on the mat. It seemed an unnecessary courtesy given that it hadn't rained for days. Helen could not wait for him to finish.

'Did Harvey send you?'

'Yes, ma'am, I've come down from Taunton.'

'Taunton? It must be important.'

'Yes, I guess it must. He called me last night in a bit of a mood.'

He stepped forward and she closed the door behind him.

'Is he all right?'

'He's okay, just not very happy.'

'What do you mean?'

'Is your phone working?

'I think so, why?' She was having difficulty concealing her mounting exasperation that he wasn't coming to the point.

'Well, he's been trying to get through to you since the weekend. You see, ma'am, he's lost his mobile phone, and he's fretting 'cos he thinks you'll be worrying your pretty head.'

He paused, and looked at her curiously. She realised that the relief on her face must be visible.

'Anyhow, I've got a number here for you. Only you'll have to call before midday, 'cos they're going to be moving on after that.'

He reached in his pocket and held out a piece of paper. She seized it from him, turned and looked at the clock. There was a little less than twenty minutes to spare. She wanted to make the call in private.

'Listen, er, Courtney, would you like a coffee?'

'That's mighty kind of you, ma'am. Can I take a look at the phone for you while you're making it?'

'It's all right, I'll use the mobile to call Harvey.'

'Okay, no problem, but I could take a look at it anyhow. I know a thing or two about phones.'

Helen hesitated a moment longer, then agreed. Maybe she could leave him to get on with that while she went upstairs to call her lover.

The kettle was still boiling, however, when Courtney came into the kitchen.

'It's fixed,' he declared. The grin seemed even broader.

'What was wrong?'

'Simple problem, really, ma'am. The extension lead had come free of the socket. I just popped it back in for you.'

She smiled and thanked him. Her mind was juggling several issues as she began to make the coffee: what to do with Courtney so that she could free herself to make the call, what to say to Harvey in the short time they would have available, and how the phone lead had been dislodged. Helen felt sure she hadn't been responsible for severing the connection; she hadn't used the home phone since the burglary, nor had she even been near where the extension lead ran. Perhaps the police who searched the room had done it accidentally; or else the intruder had done it deliberately in order to prevent the alarm from being raised.

There was a quarter of an hour to go until midday. Helen was about to address the problem of what to do with Courtney when it solved itself. As she handed him the coffee, he asked whether he might take it out into the back garden. He wanted to sit and look out over the sea while she called Harvey.

She escorted him to the seat near the rock pool, and felt butterflies in her stomach as she did so: this was where she had first kissed Harvey, and minutes later they were in the bedroom. Helen excused herself, explaining that she had better make the phone call right away. Courtney nodded. 'Now be sure to tell him he owes me one,' he called after her.

Once inside the house, Helen wasted no time. She rushed up the stairs, clutching the piece of paper which Courtney had brought with him. Closing the bedroom door behind her, she took a quick look out of the

94

window overlooking the garden. Her visitor was still where she had left him, absorbed in his contemplation of the horizon. Helen flopped face downwards onto the bed, and began to dial the number. She did not recognise the international code, and her preoccupation with what was wrong had made her lose track of where Harvey should be. A woman answered in a language she could not identify, although she thought she could make out the words 'Hotel Europa'. She was relieved to find that the woman replied in the affirmative when asked if she spoke English. Helen explained that she needed to speak to Harvey Newman and that it was urgent. There was a pause, and then the woman said she would put her through to his room.

The phone seemed to ring interminably. When finally there was an answer, it still wasn't Harvey.

'Who's that?' she asked.

'It's Neil.'

Helen remembered that Harvey had mentioned Neil in the context of a conversation about *Kosmos*.

'Are you the guitarist?'

'Sure am. Is it Harvey you're after?'

'Yes, is he there?'

'He's in the can.'

'What?'

There was a short pause.

'He means I've been having a pee.'

At last she could hear the voice she had been longing for.

'Harvey?'

'Helen, baby, where the hell have you been?

'I've been wondering where you had got to!'

'Oh. I'm in Belgium. If it's Tuesday, this must be Belgium. Oh. It's Wednesday! That means we're off to . . . where is it we're off to Neilie?'

A short pause was followed by a guffaw.

'Shlezvik Holstein! He says we're going to Schhlezzvikk Holstein. Have you heard of that, honey?'

'No.'

'No, me neither. Apparently, it's some dumper truck little place in Germany.'

'Harvey, have you been drinking?'

'No. No, no, no, no, non, non, nein, nein, no . . . Well, yes.'

'But it's not even midday.

'Over here it is! It's, let me see, now, one o'clock. Surely that makes it okay to be sozzled?'

Helen discovered that she was giggling, and realised that it was some time since she had laughed. In fact, she hadn't had a really good chuckle since Harvey had left. She could hear him mimicking her on the other end of the line.

'Oh, Harvey, why do you have to be drunk when I have so much to tell you?'

'And so little time in which to tell it. We have precisely two minutes, or should I say, "svei minuten"?'

'Oh no, do you have to go? Can't you hold on for just a little longer? I really have to talk to you.'

'No, I'm sorry my darling, but Baron von Richthofen awaits. Hey, would you believe it? The reason we're going to Schhleezzvikk Holsshtein, is that some batty Bavarian aristocrat wants us to play at his private ceremony. He's willing to pay us thousands of pounds just to do some acoustic numbers as background music to his party!'

'Harvey, please be serious for a moment.'

'Why? That's boring! Anyway, we could have talked for longer if you had been in when I rang!'

'I was in. That's what I've been trying to tell you. I've hardly been anywhere. The phone's been out of action. It's okay, now, though, Courtney's fixed it. But why didn't you ring me on my mobile?'

'Because, my precious, I don't know the number. It's stored in the index on my mobile. And my mobile, as I presume you are aware, has gone and done a runner in Amsterdam.'

'Have you reported it to the phone company?'

'I have now. At first, we thought it was in the hotel. When I rang them up the plonkers said one had just been handed in. I sent one of the roadies back to fetch it, and when he got there, it turned out the little sod wasn't mine.'

Helen finally felt assured that he had been telling the truth. She wondered whether her relief would be as obvious to Harvey as it had been to Courtney when he had first presented her with the explanation.

'So how come you haven't been out?' he continued.

'I've been worrying about you.'

'Did you think I had forgotten you?'

'I didn't know what to think.'

'What's the matter? Don't you trust me?'

'It's not that. It's just that we haven't known each other all that long and . . .'

'You need to learn to trust me' he cut in.

She was silent for a few seconds, contemplating the possibilities. Trust wasn't something that came naturally to her. On the other hand she didn't want to allow unjustified suspicions to tarnish their relationship.

'Okay,' she acknowledged eventually.

There was a pause. He seemed to be sobering up.

'So have you been missing me?' he asked quietly.

'Don't you know I have? Guess what I've been doing! I've been counting the days until you come back. I haven't done that since I was a child. I used to know how many days there were until we went on holiday, or until my next birthday. What have you done to me?'

'I've been squeezing your heart until it hurts.'

'Oh, you're such a smoothie, you're so good with words!'

'If you say so, princess. Is that all I'm good at, or can you think of anything else?'

'I don't want to.'

'No?'

'Not now.'

'Why not?'

'Because you're not here to do anything about it.'

'Have you no imagination?' Even as he spoke, she was beginning to gasp.

'Stop it.'

'What are you wearing?'

Helen rolled over onto her back before attempting to answer:

'Just a gown.'

'What colour is it?'

'Peach.'

'Hmm, sounds lovely. Okay, get rid of it!'

'Why?'

'Just do it.'

Helen wriggled free.

'Okay, I'm completely naked.'

'Good, now close your eyes.' He paused for a moment. 'Got them closed?'

'Yes.'

'Now, can you see me?'

'I can see your eyes, your gorgeous blue eyes.'

'Good. Now, put your hand where I would put mine, and touch yourself as I would touch you.'

He listened with satisfaction as she groaned.

'Can you feel me?'

'Yes . . . You're all over me.'

'Am I with you?'

'Yes, yes, you're here.'

'Good. That's good, because honey, I have to go now.'

'Oh no!'

'I don't want to, but I have to. Neil's waiting outside. We're late already.'

'But darling, I still have so much to say to you.'

'It can't be helped. Listen, I'll call you as soon as I can.'

'Oh no, don't go just yet. Can't you get them to hold on just a few more minutes?'

'Sorry, no can do. It simply wouldn't do to keep the bloody red baron waiting.'

Helen could hear a knocking sound in the background. 'I'm just coming, Neilie,' she heard him say.

'How can I contact you?' she asked.

'I'll have to call you. It won't be until tomorrow. There's no gig tomorrow night. Will you be in?'

'You bet I will.'

'Okay. Stay sexy for me. Goodbye sweetheart.'

'Bye, my love.'

He was gone. But he wasn't gone forever. Just when it had seemed all was lost she had been given a reprieve. Perhaps God did understand why she had found it necessary to do what she did, and had not forsaken her after all. Could it be that the last few days had been her sentence, and that now she had been punished she would be able to move on? Perhaps her conscience would cease to trouble her now.

Helen let go of her mobile and stretched her arms and legs until she was splayed out like starfish. She was still feeling the effects that the mere sound of his voice had on her. It was incredible how he could overwhelm her without even trying, sometimes without even noticing. Her mind went back to the moment in Andrew's kitchen, when she had been thinking about the burglary, and suddenly, inexplicably, her memory had thrown up a vivid recollection of their first experience of their passion for each other. She seemed to drift into a world of her own. She remembered leaning back on the chair, arching her back just as she had when Harvey had picked her up and laid her on his bed that first night. Suddenly she had become aware that Andrew was standing right by her. Had he noticed? Even if he had failed to spot the other symptoms, he could hardly have missed the flush which had coloured her complexion. And he must have wondered why she had gobbled up the meal he had prepared for her and made a beeline for home. She just hoped that he hadn't thought that this state of arousal had anything to do with him. She wished now that she had made her apology more specific, but what was she supposed to say? 'Oh, Andrew, sorry I was feeling so turned on when I was sitting in your kitchen. I hope it wasn't too obvious. Don't worry, it was nothing to do with you.'

Sounds of life coming from below interrupted her train of thought. First a door closed, then a cup clanked against the metal of the kitchen sink. With a sigh, Helen put her gown back on and hurried down the staircase. Courtney was hovering in the hall.

'You know, ma'am, you are so lucky living here.'

'So you liked the view.'

'I sure did ma'am. I could have stayed there all day, just staring at those waves coming in, and all those people in their wetsuits trying to stay on their surfboards.'

'Why don't you stop a bit longer?' Even as she spoke she was hoping that he would decline the offer.

'I would love to, ma'am, truly I would, but I must be getting back. I have a gig on this evening.'

'What do you play?'

'Me, I play sax,' he replied, grinning even more widely at the expression of interest. 'Tenor, alto, bass, baritone, soprano. You name them, I play them.'

'What kind of music?'

'Jazz mostly, but I play all kinds of music.'

She was looking at him curiously.

'You're not . . . Courtney Pine?'

He began to laugh heartily.

'No, ma'am. Courtney Saunders, at your service.' He raised his hand to his cap. Helen did her best to hide her embarrassment.

'I must remember to tell Harvey that!' he went on.

'Oh, please don't!'

He drew his breath and managed to control his mirth. His face retained its cheeky look.

'You know, ma'am, Harvey said something very sweet to me last night. He said he wished it was me who was out there touring with them. He said the sax player who's with them now is . . . well, I guess I better not use the exact words in front of a lady.'

Helen smiled, but was concerned at this latest indication that the tour was encountering problems.

'Did you tell him he owes me one?' Courtney went on.

'Oh yes, and he said to thank you very much for your help,' she replied, reluctant to acknowledge her omission.

'Good, well it's been a joy to meet you, ma'am. I hope I'll see you again sometime.'

'It's been a pleasure, Courtney' she said, opening the door for him. 'And please, call me Helen.'

He raised his cap again as he passed her.

'Goodbye, ma'am . . . er, Helen.'

She watched him until he was halfway down the path. Suddenly she could wait no longer and closed the door. She turned, looked up to the ceiling, and said aloud: 'Thank you, God.'

Closing her eyes, she found she could picture Harvey. Her fingers were loosening the ribbon around her gown. If only he were here now, he would chase her up to the bedroom. She began to skip up the stairs, two at a time. Pausing one step short of the landing, she opened up the gown as wide as it would go, like a peacock spreading its wings. Then she allowed it to tumble down her back. A deft flick of the foot enabled her to catch it momentarily on her heel. As she kicked it back down the steps, she imagined it dropping neatly over Harvey's head. She squealed with delight at the thought of teasing him like that. He would pretend to be enraged. He would insist that she deserved a good spanking and that it was down to him to punish her . . .

Helen flung herself on the bed, panting slightly. She drew her legs up underneath her so that she was curled up in a ball of desire. A smile spread across her face. Even if she went back to work tomorrow, she had the whole of the rest of the day in which to titillate herself, to dream idly of her lover, to imagine how they would frolic together when he came back. And now she believed that he really would be coming back to her. Suddenly her smile turned to a giggle as it dawned on her that she had completely overlooked something during their conversation. She had been so taken up with the reassurance he was giving her, and then so alive with the passion he inspired in her, that it had slipped her mind altogether. She rolled over onto her back and continued to chuckle at the realisation that she hadn't even mentioned the burglary.

Chapter 17

Just as Gareth tapped the knocker he heard a clock within strike seven o'clock. It was exactly two weeks since he had first confronted Helen about the affair. This evening was a chance to take his mind off his predicament, and at least attempt to enjoy himself. Earlier in the week it had been Megan who had issued the invitation: 'Mummy wants you to come to dinner on Friday.' At first he had not taken her seriously, but later when Jenny came out to hang up the washing she had repeated the offer, and he had felt obliged to accept.

He did not have to wait on the doorstep for long. Megan let him in, skipped down the hallway, and ushered him into the lounge. Jenny was just putting the finishing touches to the table, neatly set for three, with the fourth side against the wall just under the window overlooking the back garden. She turned and beamed at him. It was the same look that Megan gave him whenever her head appeared over the hedge.

He held up the bottle of Chilean Chardonnay he had brought with him.

'Ooh!' she greeted him. 'Told you there was no need, see.'

He protested that it was only fair that he should contribute something.

'But mother, didn't you say we were having champagne?'

'That's right, maid, but we can have both.'

Gareth looked puzzled. Had he overlooked something?

'I got new job,' Jenny explained. 'Not goin' nowhere though.'

'That's great.' He forced a smile. Megan had taken him by the hand and was leading him towards the table.

'Mother wants you to sit in the middle.'

Jenny giggled inexplicably. 'I'm going to be head cleaner,' she added.

Gareth found he was sitting down now, with Megan to his right, leaving the seat nearest the kitchen door free. Jenny sniffed, looked worried, then turned and scurried through the doorway.

'So what have you been doing today, Megan?'

'We've been to the Charlie Dimmock exhibition.'

'Where was that?'

'In court.'

'Where? In Bodmin?'

'Yes.'

Gareth continued to look bemused for some seconds. Then he realised what she was talking about.

'You mean the Charlotte Dymond experience.'

Megan thought for a moment.

'That's what I said,' she asserted, grinning.

'No, you're confusing two different people. Charlie Dimmock is the one who appears on the gardening programmes on the television.'

'Her wears no bra,' Jenny called out from the kitchen.

'You're thinking of Charlotte Dymond. She was murdered on the moor in the nineteenth century, and they hung a man for it. Only I don't think they're so sure it was him now.'

'That's right!' Megan held an arm aloft in her excitement, as though eager to answer a question in class. Then she allowed it to drop, and began to see the funny side of her misunderstanding. Soon she was giggling uncontrollably. Jenny came in, carrying the first of the plates. She too was laughing over the confusion. Even Gareth found their hilarity contagious.

'Mr Bell, Mummy says you're a very clever man,' whispered Megan after her mother had gone back to fetch the remaining dishes.

'Oh, she's being kind.'

Megan shook her head solemnly.

'No, Mr Bell, Mummy's right. Jimmy says so too.'

Gareth looked at her curiously. He had talked to Megan several times over the hedge that week and she had not mentioned her imaginary playmate since she had contrived his capture at the hands of the 'wazzock'. He had wondered whether the episode was an indication that she had outgrown the need for artificial companionship.

He went to open his mouth, but she anticipated his question.

'Jimmy's back.' She smiled triumphantly. 'I rescued him myself.'

'And the wazzock?'

Megan shrugged her shoulders.

'Gone.'

If only adult problems could be solved so simply, thought Gareth. He returned her smile in the hope of disguising the sadness prompted by this thought.

Megan appeared dissatisfied with the extent of his curiosity.

'It was easy,' she continued, nodding sagely. 'I just prayed really hard.'

Jenny came in, deposited a couple of dishes in the middle of the table, and went back into the kitchen. She returned carrying another dish in one hand and a corkscrew in the other. She invited Gareth to open the bottle of wine. Noticing her daughter's eager face she said firmly:

'You 'ave yer orange juice, maid.'

Gareth was beginning to feel concerned about the amount of food which was arriving. He had explained when he had accepted their offer that he didn't eat much. He was getting the impression that he had spoken in vain.

'Mr Bell,' Megan began quietly.

'Why not call me Uncle Gareth?'

'No, you're Mr Bell,' she asserted, 'because you're a teacher and you're clever.'

'Okay,' he conceded.

She looked at him earnestly.

'Have you ever prayed that Auntie Helen will come back like Jimmy did?'

'Yes, my dear, I have.'

Gareth realised that he had called his little neighbour 'my dear' without even thinking about it. It was the way he might have addressed a favourite niece.

There was a pause while Megan analysed his response.

'Were you in church?' she wanted to know.

Gareth shook his head. He had never felt the inclination to attend church regularly.

'That's it, then,' she concluded. 'If you weren't in church it doesn't count.'

Jenny arrived with the last of the food, and returned moments later with their plates.

'I bin keepin' 'm lovely 'n' hot,' she assured them.

Gareth's concerns about the quantity of food proved well founded. With the stew she had cooked Jenny had prepared an unnecessarily large selection of vegetables: carrots, parsnips, cauliflower, broccoli and courgettes.

'I know'd 'ee lost some weight, see' she explained.

Gareth struggled through as much as he could, but Megan and her mother were both ready for second helpings while his plate was still half full. The wine bottle, on the other hand, was almost empty. Gareth said he was glad that his choice had obviously met with Jenny's approval. She went to answer, hiccuped instead, and both she and her daughter had a fit of the giggles. When they had calmed down, Megan suddenly remembered something she had been meaning to say.

'Mr Bell, we saw a car with my name on.'

'Did you really?'

'Yes, except they spelt it M-e-g-a-n-e, which is wrong. My name is spelt M-e-g-a-n.'

Gareth smiled at her kindly.

'There's quite a few of them around,' he observed. 'They're made by a company called Renault.'

'You see, I said you were clever,' she concluded.

Gareth forced himself to keep smiling, but in reality he was beginning to feel sick, and eventually he had to abandon his attempt to clear his plate.

106

'I'm sorry, it's not that I didn't like it. It's just that I've got out of the habit of eating an evening meal.'

'Poor boy.' Jenny looked at him sympathetically. 'I know what 'ee be goin' through,' she added, patting him on the wrist as she picked up his plate.

She returned with the desserts. Gareth was grateful to see that she had prepared something runny, although he was not particularly partial to tapioca. As he put down his spoon he realised he could no longer see the bottom of the garden through the window. The evenings really were beginning to draw in.

Jenny went out to the kitchen and returned with the champagne. She passed it to Gareth and asked him to open it.

'Are you sure you want to? I mean, we probably won't get through much of it.'

'Oh, garn with 'ee. I bought it special. I'll cheer 'ee up 's evenin'.'

'Can't I try some?' Megan asked eagerly.

'You be too young.'

'Oh, please.'

'I told 'ee no.'

Megan looked crestfallen.

'Jimmy drinks champagne,' she muttered to herself. From that moment on she became subdued, as if by way of protest at this discrimination. The mixture of wine and champagne seemed to invigorate her mother, however, and she started to chatter incessantly. Soon it was nine o'clock, prompting Jenny to remind her daughter that it would soon be bedtime.

There was no complaint; indeed, within a few minutes Megan yawned and announced that it was now past her bedtime.

'Be off to bed 'n' take yer book,' Jenny urged her.

'It's up there already.'

'Off 'ee go, then.'

'Thank you for coming, Mr Bell,' she said sweetly as she left the table.

'Goodnight Megan, sleep well.'

She turned to her mother.

'Go on up, maid. I'll tuck 'ee in d'reckly.'

Megan paused as she reached the doorway.

'Thank you for the wine, Mr Bell. Maybe I'll have some another time.'

She didn't wait for a reply, but hurried off up the stairs.

'See you in the garden tomorrow,' she sang out as she reached the landing.

Noticing that Jenny's champagne glass was empty, Gareth offered to pour her some more.

''Ee'll be getting me tipsy,' she replied, but she accepted anyway.

'Megan's such a good-natured child,' Gareth observed.

Jenny nodded proudly.

'She's my little precious.'

Gareth looked to his right. The young trees in the back garden had become silhouettes against the cool blue sky.

Jenny followed his gaze. ''Tis gettin' dark out there.' She stood up. 'Let's go sit on the sofa. 'Tis cosier over there.'

Gareth followed her to the front part of the lounge. Megan had left the door open. Jenny closed it as she passed by. It occurred to Gareth that perhaps there was more to the invitation than had met the eye. He wondered whether Megan's readiness to go to bed was no coincidence.

Two large cushions at either end of the sofa narrowed the available seating space. Gareth perched on the edge of the seat.

''Ee don't look too comfy,' Jenny commented as she stood over him. 'Why not sit back a bit?' He leaned back and tried to settle into the corner, but the cushion obstructed him.

Jenny giggled. 'I'll take that out yer way.' She leaned across him and tugged at the corner of the cushion. She was wearing a sandy coloured summer dress, held up by thin shoulder straps. When she was upright, there was just a hint of cleavage, but now, as Gareth sat forward slightly to free the cushion, he found himself staring at her navel. He was reminded of her earlier remark about Charlie Dimmock.

'There, that's better,' she said as she stood up. It wasn't obvious what to do with the cushion. She tossed it playfully into the opposite corner of the room and plonked herself down beside him.

''Ope you're havin' a good time,' she smiled.

'Yes, thanks.' He returned her smile, then looked away, feigning interest in the ornaments which lined the shelf above the fireplace.

'That's good, then, 'cos I know just what you're goin' through. 'Twas the same for me when Ray upped and left. I never felt so low in me whole life. I've been so lonely since.' She paused. Gareth was aware that she was looking directly at him, and found himself returning her gaze. He could see that tears were forming in her eye. 'Course, young Megan really misses havin' her father around' she continued, 'though I can't truly say he was that good to her. What she really needs is a proper man like yourself around the 'ouse.'

Gareth looked uncertainly at her, questioning his understanding of what she was saying. She reached out and patted his knee, allowed her hand to rest there for a moment, and then squeezed his leg gently. He was no longer in any doubt. It had come completely out of the blue, but he was being offered a way out.

'I wanted 'ee to come round 'ere so we could get to know each other better.' She began massaging the upper part of his leg. Gareth made no attempt to stop her. Although he was enjoying her gentle touch, he was only partially conscious of his pleasure. He was far more aware of his surprise at the turn of events.

'I've always 'ad a soft spot for 'ee,' Jenny confessed. Her hand came to rest tantalisingly on the top of his thigh. It was as though she was waiting for permission before going any further. Gareth continued to gawp at her. His mouth was open, but he was too stunned to think of anything to say.

Jenny's face was a rosy glow, a mixture of desire and embarrassment at her admission. Her chest was moving up and down quite rapidly, and he could hear her breathing. One of the straps had slipped off and was flopping by her elbow, and Gareth's eyes were drawn to her bare shoulder. Facially, Jenny was nothing like Helen. She had a larger mouth, chubbier cheeks and brown eyes. What's more Jenny's hair was short, dark and curly. But their bodies were quite similar: they had the same skin texture, shapely figure and prominent breasts. And now as he stared at Jenny's shoulder it seemed as though he were seeing Helen again.

Noticing the direction of his gaze, Jenny grinned. Emboldened, she began caressing his leg again. Leaning towards him, she whispered in his ear: 'Do 'ee wanna see more?'

She let go of his leg, placed her hand under his chin, and drew his face towards hers. His mouth was open, but it wasn't ready for the kiss that she initiated. Rather he was beginning to recover his powers of expression.

'Wait,' he managed to say, turning his head to one side until his ear was where his mouth had been a moment earlier. Undeterred, Jenny pointed her tongue and began to moisten the lobe. Gareth pulled away, but when he saw the look of hurt surprise on her face he put his arms round her and pulled her towards him. She linked her hands behind his back, and they remained in this silent embrace for some seconds.

'This is all a bit sudden,' Gareth whispered eventually. 'I mean, I had no idea you felt like this.'

'Don't yer like me, then?' she wanted to know.

He let go of her and moved back, so that he was able to look her in the eyes. He wanted her to know that he was being honest. He was experiencing a conflict. His body was responding to her proximity, but his heart and mind were holding him back.

'It's not that; the thing is, it's only two weeks since Helen left.'

'But how long is it since you last 'ad some nooky? Must be longer 'n that.'

'Yes, but not much. Anyway that's not the point.'

She eyed him curiously. It was another look that Megan had inherited.

'I'n't you hungry then?'

He showed some amusement at the expression.

'That's what Ray 'd call it. 'Ee'd tell me 'e was hungry.'

Gareth sensed a chance to back up his argument.

'You see, you still think about Ray a lot, and that was a year ago.'

She paused for thought.

'So 'ow long d'yer reckon it'll take 'ee?'

He looked away now, not wanting even to contemplate the answer to that question, let alone try to impart it to anyone else. Yet neither his eyes nor his mind could focus on anything else. The pain in his heart was beginning to throb. He wondered whether it might go away once he had given Jenny her answer.

Somehow he found the courage to look her in the eye again.

'I don't know that I ever will.'

Gareth saw Jenny's face fall; his reply had dashed any lingering hopes of passion. Now it was her turn to look away. He began to push his body forward; she unclasped her hands and allowed him to stand. He looked through the gloomy front garden and saw that the moon was almost a perfect circle, perching just above the moor. But it was going to waste, at least as far as they were concerned.

'I'm gonna go say g'night to me baby,' he heard Jenny say.

'Okay,' he replied. 'Listen, I had better go.' He looked over his shoulder and saw that she was on her feet, and nearing the door. Her face had gone very red, and even from a distance it was obvious she was struggling to hold back the tears.

'I'll let myself out,' he went on, stealing one last glance at the dusky sky as he spoke. 'And thank you for the . . . '

But already he could hear her footsteps on the stairs.

Chapter 18

It was the sound of crying that woke Gareth up. He checked the time: it was half past midnight. It must have been about three hours ago that he had come in to an empty home, staggered up to the bedroom, and collapsed onto the bed without bothering to undress. He sat up and tried to identify the source of the lamentation. His first thought was that it was Jenny who was crying, but as he listened carefully he realised that he was hearing the same sound which had disturbed him the night Helen moved out. Again he made his way to the top of the stairs, but this time he made no attempt to bring an end to his little neighbour's distress. He did not feel able to offer her any words of reassurance; on the contrary, he felt that he was responsible for her tears. For whom was Megan crying, he wondered? Herself? Her mother? Him? All of them? Whatever the answer, he felt sure he would be unable to help. Indeed, all he wanted was to get away from the sound of her sobs. So he hurried downstairs, switched on the television, and turned the volume up. The remote control was slow to operate; Gareth remembered that he had been meaning to replace the batteries. Somehow each time he had gone shopping he had overlooked this. As he struggled to change the channel he cursed his forgetfulness. If Helen had been around, she would have moaned at him for not having achieved something so straightforward.

There was little to choose between the channels: Gareth decided to wait and see what would follow the adverts on the local network. In the meantime he reached for his journal. He wanted to record a thought which had crossed his mind earlier in the day. He would begin with this, and leave any reflections on what had occurred while he was next door for later, perhaps for another day. He opened the book and wrote:

Friday 9th August

It struck me this afternoon while in the garden that I have to accept that contentment is a thing of the past. If I could pass on one recommendation to everyone who knows me it would be this: Relish every moment of happiness. You never know when it will be your last.

The television suddenly went quiet; the adverts had finished and a pink caption on a bright blue background announced the resumption of the programme they had interrupted: '*Rock am Fest 2002*'. This meant nothing to Gareth, who waited to see what would follow. He realised he could hear the sound of a solo violin, set against the background of an unlit stage. Alerted to the possibility of some sort of classical music recital, he put the journal down on the floor and sat back in the chair. He listened intently for around half a minute. The piece was jaunty; there was a hint of 'For he's a jolly good fellow' about the melody – until without warning the pitch went up dramatically, and the single violinist rapidly turned into a whole string ensemble, all bowing frantically, creating an unsavoury cacophony. Then all hell broke loose.

The notion that this was some form of classical concert suddenly went out of the window as a frenzy of electronic sound erupted. Conscious that the noise would be audible in the other half of the cottage, Gareth seized the remote control and pressed the arrow key to reduce the volume. On this occasion the gadget responded promptly. Although he was not given to watching the pop music programmes which were a feature of late-night television, the contrast between the opening bars and what followed had intrigued him, and he found himself scanning the screen in an attempt to ascertain what instruments were involved in this assault on his eardrums. He could see through the colourful smoke which now billowed from various corners of the stage that at least three guitarists and a keyboard player were contributing energetically to the apparent disarray: he could also make out two percussionists in the background. Several minutes elapsed before there was any sign of respite. Gareth was surprised to note that one of the guitars now reprised the melody which the violins introduced, although it was apparent from the harsher tone that it was something of a parody of the original tune. He reflected that he hadn't realised that such sophistication was a feature of this sort of music. As the guitar faded, a solitary figure emerged through the smoke. He wasn't carrying a guitar, or any other instrument. Only when he held up the microphone and began to sing did a spotlight pick him out. It was clear that he was talented: every note was precise and every syllable was clearly pronounced. His voice, in fact, seemed strangely familiar, and as the camera zoomed in on the singer Gareth focused on his face in an effort to identify him . . .

It was only when the camera came really close that Gareth finally realised who it was. When the connection was made it jolted him into action, and he reached once again for the remote control, seeking urgently to change the channel so as to be rid of the image. But this time the response was slow, and the song ended while Gareth was still waiting for something to happen. Still Gareth persevered with the uncooperative gadget, determined not to let it beat him.

'That was called "My Playmate Stabbed Me",' Harvey announced to the cheering crowd. 'Now we're gonna give you "No More Promises".' Gareth abandoned the channel-change key in favour of the off switch, and was holding the controller at various angles in the hope of making a connection; but still there was nothing. The title of the song he had just heard was resounding in his head: My Playmate Stabbed Me, indeed! How dare the man sing about betrayal, when he himself had caused a wife to deceive her husband? Gareth felt a wave of resentment starting to swell inside him. He turned his attention to the volume-down arrow, and finally succeeded in silencing his oppressor. But now, in stark contrast to the previous song, the camera's focus was entirely on the singer's face, and those penetrating eyes seemed to be returning Gareth's gaze. And still the remote was refusing to put an end to this torture. A tacit moment in the vocal part afforded Harvey the chance to nod knowingly, and a smug grin appeared on his face as he stretched his arm out and wagged a finger. Even this action somehow oozed self-satisfaction and intimidation. Yes, Gareth, I am having a really good time at your expense. I am enjoying humiliating you, mocking you, tormenting you . . .

All at once the smirk was too broad, the finger was pointed once too often, the revulsion was just too overwhelming.

'Bloody wazzock!' Gareth shouted, suddenly heedless of the way that sound carried through the walls.

The useless gadget was somersaulting high in the air behind Gareth's chair. It narrowly missed the lampshade in the middle of the ceiling, and fell just short of the front window, skidding to a halt near the corner where Joey used to be.

It was the television which felt the main impact of Gareth's outburst. A heavy hand scored a direct hit on the face in the centre of the screen. The television toppled backwards off its stand, landed with a hefty thud on the stone floor behind it, and gave up the ghost without a splutter of protest.

'There,' declared Gareth, too jubilant about the blow he had struck against his adversary to be concerned about the pain in his fingers or the irreparable damage he had done to the set. 'I never want to see you again. Never . . . ever . . . ever!'

Chapter 19

Helen lay slowly back until her hair cushioned her head against the enamel. Everything in the bathroom was the same colour: the ceiling, the walls, the basin, the tiling, and even the liquid in which she was immersed. All were as white as a bridal gown. As pure as the relationship was impure. Helen scolded whichever wayward part of her mind had brought that thought to the surface, and allowed her body to savour the sticky substance with which it was surrounded.

'So how come its quite warm in places?' she enquired, when she was finally ready to emerge from this state of inertia.

There was no answer. She sat up, and watched some of the liquid run down her breasts and arms. Reluctantly she pushed on the sides of the bath, and levered herself upright. She looked in the mirror, saw more white than flesh, and giggled.

'Where are you?' she called, but again there was no response. She reached for the towel, but instead of wiping her body with it she laid it out on the floor between the bath and the door, and used it as a means of protecting the floor from the inevitable drips. A moment later she was standing in the open doorway.

'Oh sorry', she said, 'I didn't realise you were on the phone.' But even as she spoke, he was replacing the receiver.

Harvey sat naked on the edge of the bed. For a few seconds he stared in her direction. The look on his face was serious and distant. She was about to seek an explanation, but he spoke first:

'I topped it up with some hot milk.'

'How did you manage that?'

'I had to buy a portable stove and some saucepans specially.' He nodded in the direction of the corner of the bedroom. 'It was worth it, though.'

Helen tiptoed towards the bed, trying to avoid leaving too many splodges on the carpet. The grin returned to Harvey's face.

'Did you drink any of it?'

'I had a little sip. What sort of yoghurt was it?'

'Greek, with some fruit.'

'I came across a whole banana,' she chuckled. 'Harvey, that must have taken you ages to empty all those pots into that bath like that.'

He nodded.

'I thought a hundred might be enough, but it wasn't. I had to go back for more.'

'How did you know I've always fantasised about bathing in yoghurt?'

He shrugged his shoulders.

'I didn't.'

She sat down beside him and began to explore the thick mat of hair on his chest.

'Harvey, I couldn't believe it when you sent me the plane tickets. It was the sweetest thing you could possibly have done. And now this bath . . . Are there any more surprises?'

'No, that's it for now.'

'Did you know I've never been to Paris?'

He shook his head. Her fingers were straying down past his navel. She purred as they reached their destination.

'I've always wanted to come here. And now that I have, I'm not even going to see any of it.'

He covered one of her cheeks with the palm of his hand and turned her head towards him. There was a twinkle in his eyes as he spoke:

'You mean you wouldn't rather do some sight-seeing?'

She laughed heartily, put her arms around him and pushed him backwards onto the bed. Then she sat astride him and thought for a moment.

'There's no way I'm going out there. I wouldn't be able to concentrate, anyway. People would ask me when I got back what I had seen and I'd have to tell them I had no idea.'

She fell face down on top of him so that she could look him in the eyes from the closest possible range.

'I want us to spend every moment we can together, just like this.'

The anticipated look of delight did not materialise, and Helen was reminded of the question she had wanted to ask:

'Harvey, what's wrong?' She pressed down on the bed on either side of him, pushing her body upwards so that she could see his face clearly.

He seemed reluctant to answer, and evaded her gaze, absorbing himself instead in her dangling breasts.

'It's not important,' he replied, just in time to prevent Helen from losing her patience. 'Not compared to us.'

'But whatever it is, it's stopping us from making the most of our time together. And we only have the rest of this evening, and tomorrow night after the gig.'

Harvey shook his head, as he looked up at her:

'Not even tomorrow night. I'll be so high on adrenaline, I won't be able to think of anything else, not even you. There's always Sunday morning, though. Your plane doesn't leave until two.'

He saw how crestfallen she looked, and forced a smile. This did not satisfy Helen. She clambered off him, lay down beside him on her back, and drew the duvet cover up over them both. Harvey remained where he was, absorbed in silent contemplation.

Helen wondered whether he might be more responsive now that she wasn't looking down on him in such an intimidating manner. She decided to chance her arm:

'Who was that on the phone?'

'It wasn't another woman, if that's what you're thinking.'

'Did I say that?'

'No, but can you put your hand on your heart and tell me it hadn't crossed your mind?'

She was silent.

Suddenly Harvey seemed to burst into life. He sat up quickly, and now it was his turn to look down on her:

'All right, damn it, I'll tell you, since it's obviously so important to you. I'll tell you the whole humiliating truth. That was Ginger, the band manager.'

'I know, you've talked about him. Ginger, as in ginger beer . . .'

'Yes, that's the fella. And no, in case you're wondering, there's nothing going on between me and him.'

She laughed nervously.

'Ginger doesn't do much that's useful, but he does keep an eye on how well our performances are going down in the press. He tells me we're being upstaged by the support band. Imagine that! Some two-bit Italian boy band that nobody's ever heard of are stealing all our headlines.'

'Is there anything you can do about it?'

'Well, we could all try to look twenty years younger. Or we could learn to prance around on the stage like Wayne Sleep.'

She sniggered: Harvey remained straight-faced.

'The trouble is *Kosmos* is not a happy band. Our regular saxophonist is sick, and we're having to use a stand-in, and he's just not on the same planet as the rest of us. The real problem, though, is Stig.'

He saw from her frown that she was struggling to remember.

'The keyboardist,' he informed her, a little vexation apparent in his voice. 'The thing is, he's satisfied with what we've achieved already. Okay, we're quite well known at the moment, but will anyone play our music in twenty or a thirty years time? I want us to go on and become a super group, like the Beatles or Abba. And the music we play is good enough, it really is.'

Helen watched him closely as his frustration mounted. There was an intensity about him which was almost spellbinding.

'People have been telling me since I was a teenager that it was very difficult to break through in the music industry. I've known that all along. I always tell them that I'm better at difficult things than easy things. It took fifteen years of hard work before at last I wrote a song which really made our name.'

Helen smiled:

'*I cried a tear for you*,' she affirmed. 'I remember when it came out. They played it on the radio a lot. I knew all the words. Still do.'

'If I didn't know better I'd accuse you of hero worship.' Still his expression was serious. He was wrestling to find a way of capturing an image which would convey what he was trying to say. Suddenly he found one:

'It's as though we've climbed Mount Everest, and fifty yards short of the top we've stopped to admire the view, and Stig wants to stay there for a little while, and then go back down again.'

Helen thought for a moment, then asked:

'Couldn't you go on to the top without him?'

Harvey shook his head:

'I wish I could. But it's not as simple as that. Our best songs have been the ones where there's been some input from Stig. I can write the lyrics and the melodies, but I can't write accompaniments as well as Stig can. He has the ability to round things off. I've tried getting other people to do it, but they just don't do it to the same standard. The trouble is he has to be in a creative frame of mind, whereas I can just get on with it whenever I want to. That means there's always a backlog of work. At the moment I have about ten songs - enough to make an album - just waiting for him to pull his finger out.'

'Isn't there some way you could get him to do more?'

'I've tried. But if I put too much pressure on him he becomes uncooperative and gets even less done. Half the time I can't even get in contact with him. He spends a lot of time fishing and refuses to take his mobile with him. I bet he's out there now, dangling his rod in the Seine.'

Helen tried in vain to stifle a little giggle. She sensed a hint of reproach in the look he gave her.

'I've told myself many times I've got to learn to make light of it. But I can't help feeling frustrated. We have the chance to get our names into the history books and we may be about to squander it because our star keyboardist is more interested in getting his dinner on the end of a hook.'

Helen rolled over until her breast came to rest on Harvey's rib cage. Her tongue began to tickle his cheek with little circular movements.

'You said the wrong thing there,' she whispered.

'Eh?'

'You were talking about feeling frustrated. I've had three weeks of that.' She paused for thought. 'Actually I've had twenty years of that.'

She got up and sat astride him again. This time there was a grin so broad that Harvey couldn't help mirroring it.

Helen wagged her finger at him as he started to groan.

'I didn't come all this way just to carry on feeling frustrated.'

She brought her mouth down on top of his, and his half-hearted attempts to protest ceased abruptly.

Helen remembered the beginning and the end. The beginning had been atmospheric, and recognisable as the tune from the BT advert. The end had been dramatic - a feverish crescendo of woodwind, brass and tympani, which was so compelling that it threatened to detract from the pinnacle of togetherness which they had just reached. Helen knew little about classical music; however, she understood enough about Harvey to realise that he had succeeded in coordinating the moment of their mutual ecstasy with the climax of this orchestral masterpiece.

'So what was that, anyway?' Helen wanted to know.

'That was the best experience of my entire life. It's all downhill from here.'

She giggled, uncertain as to whether to believe him. He glanced over his shoulder as he stood up and made his way to the bathroom. Once more, there was a suggestion of annoyance in his look, and she wished she had kept her uncertainty to herself. She watched him as he padded across the carpet, feasting her eyes on his firm, fleshy buttocks.

He paused as he reached the door, turned and looked at her.

121

'Since you ask, it was *Daphnis et Chloé*, by Ravel. Just right for Paris, don't you think?'

He didn't wait for a reply. Helen rolled over onto her front, and fumbled for her watch. Her dismay at the realisation that it was nearly 11.00 a.m. was compounded by the sound of the shower starting up. So that was it, then: there would be no more lovemaking for another sixteen days. They would be sixteen joyless, wasted days. If she had the power she would prefer to simply turn the clock forward to Tuesday 3rd September.

Harvey returned with a white towel wrapped around him. In an attempt to raise both their spirits she pounced on him from behind and tried to wrest it from him, but he managed to wriggle free. Helen sat naked on the edge of the bed and studied him as he finished drying himself. Once more the look on his face was stern and intense. She wondered whether his mind was starting to switch to the performance which was due to round off the French leg of the tour later that day. She tried to think of something - anything at all - which would get his attention back for their last hour together.

'Oh, I've been meaning to tell you, I've brought the budgie over. You don't mind, do you? It was just that after the burglary I wanted some sort of life about the place.'

He was starting to get dressed.

'I'm not that keen on pets,' he said absent-mindedly.

'Do you want me to take him back?'

'No,' he said simply, without looking at her.

Helen flopped onto her back and looked forlornly at him.

'Harvey,' she began plaintively.

He finished buttoning his shirt, and turned towards the mirror, comb in hand. When she had summoned up the nerve to continue, Helen made no attempt to conceal her malaise:

'Harvey, did you mean what you said just now?'

At last she had his attention. He was looking at her in the mirror. She saw that he was nodding gravely.

'You'll leave me sooner or later,' he said. 'Nothing this good ever lasts. And since I'm not about to end it, it follows that you will be the one who leaves me.'

Helen sat up suddenly.

'No,' she said indignantly.

He was looking at her intently now.

'So, prove me wrong then. Tell me you're happy.'

She hesitated.

'Well, there you are then,' he observed forlornly. She ignored his remark, and eventually found her answer:

'I would be if I didn't feel so bloody guilty all the time.'

He turned and looked directly at her, as if searching for the slightest indication of deceit.

'What about you?' she asked. 'Are you happy?'

He fixed his eyes on hers. His expression didn't change at all.

'I can't be happy if you're not.'

Helen sensed that he meant it. She stood up, stepped forward and cradled his head between her breasts.

'Haven't you ever experienced real happiness?'

Harvey pulled his head away and looked up at her.

'Only enough to know what I'm missing.'

Helen gazed at him sorrowfully. She wanted to know what lay behind his response, to understand what his problems had been, to see whether there was anything she could do to help him. Harvey smiled ruefully, before concluding:

'I think even if a time came when everything that's important to me was just as it should be I still couldn't be happy. I would still be too busy wondering how long it would be until the next thing went wrong.'

Helen continued to stare down at him. There was so much she wanted to say, but she didn't know how to begin. All at once she wanted to reassure him, encourage him, look after him. Her concern must have been apparent in her face, because his expression finally softened, and he took her hand and kissed it gently. Then he stood up and held her to him. They remained motionless for perhaps a minute, savouring each other's proximity, trying to suppress the thought of the taxi which had been ordered for midday. Helen decided to put aside her desire to know more about her lover's troubles.

'I had better put some clothes on,' she said eventually. She began to turn away, but Harvey raised his hand to her chin and lifted her head until her eyes couldn't avoid his gaze. The intensity in his eyes was almost alarming. Finally he asked:

'Would you marry me?'

Helen laughed nervously.

'I'm already married, remember.'

'I said *would* you, not *will* you.'

Helen found herself speechless again. Harvey dropped his hand and turned his back on her.

'I just thought I would find out where I stood - how serious you really were about me. After all, you had little hesitation about moving into my house.'

'Oh, Harvey, I am serious, all right? It's just that we've been together for such a short time. Even if I were free, it would be too soon for such a commitment, don't you think? Just now it was you who was saying that nothing this good could last!'

Harvey sighed, returned to the mirror and retrieved his comb. Helen's fingers had ruffled his hair so much that he had to start again.

'I suppose you're right,' he conceded eventually. 'And as you say, it's an academic question. You're someone else's wife.'

'Oh, please don't say it like that. It sounds so cold and hard.'

'Unpalatable truths generally are cold and hard.'

'But there's no need to rub it in. And anyway, don't you think I feel bad enough already, without you reminding me of how terribly I've let him down?'

Harvey studied her face in the mirror.

'I think you care about Gareth more than you like to admit.'

'Well, of course I care about him.'

'I don't think you really know how much you care about him. I think it's easier for me to realise than it is for you.'

Helen's face was turning red. She stepped back, sat on the bed, and buried her head in her hands. Harvey remained where he was, carefully greasing his hair into position.

'You know, I wish I could share your guilt,' he said softly. 'After all, I'm as responsible as you are for making the poor old sod's life a misery. But I don't feel guilty . . . not at all. That's not normal, is it?' He shrugged. 'But then that's me . . . I'm not normal.'

He stood up, walked over to her, and put his hand on her shoulder.

'Come on, sweetheart, I really think you ought to start getting dressed now.'

Chapter 20

It had come as a surprise to Gareth to discover that there was another service in the evening. Having cursed himself for being unable to wake up in time that Sunday morning, he had summoned up the energy to walk down and check what time the services began, with the intention of making sure he got there the following week. Finding himself in the middle of a little trickle of worshippers, he had drifted into the church. In reality Gareth had paid little attention to the service itself. His presence at the evening service did not owe itself to the desire to give thanks or praise, but to the faintest of hopes instilled by the comments of his little neighbour about the inefficacy of prayer away from church. Her words had sprung to mind many times since she had spoken them over a week beforehand, and although he still did not believe it was going to make any difference, he had concluded that if there was a chance in a thousand that it would, he would rather take it. If nothing else he would avoid spending the rest of his life wondering what difference it might have made had he turned to his maker for assistance in this, his darkest hour. He would have preferred to have the church to himself, to have made his supplications in total privacy, to have spoken aloud without anyone around to look at him curiously. But he knew that the door was kept locked following an act of vandalism some years earlier. So he settled for the next best thing - a quiet corner at the back of the church, from where the line of sight of the pulpit was obscured by a pillar. With the vicar blotted out, and the rest of the small congregation several rows in front of him, Gareth was afforded enough seclusion to concentrate on the task in hand. Wanting to feel more at home with his surroundings, he looked around at the empty wooden seats, at the faded painting on the ceiling high above him, and the murky aisle to his left. For some time he gazed across the church towards the stained glass windows, slightly cracked in places, yet beautifully illuminated by the evening sunshine.

Gareth waited until there were prayers so that he could mirror the pose adopted by the congregation, then he buried his head in his hands, and rested his elbows on his knees. Closing his eyes, he tried to bring to mind a picture of a benevolent looking figure with a reassuring face, listening carefully to his requests, reassuring him that there was nothing unreasonable about wanting your wife back, and agreeing with a nod of a wise, old head to work the necessary miracle. Gareth only had one thing to ask, so he simply began to repeat it over and over again: 'Please God, make Helen come home, please bring her back to me . . . '

Such was his concentration on this activity that Gareth began to wonder how he would bring it to an end even when he wanted to - a thought which provoked the alarming suggestion that he was becoming obsessive. However, the vicar unwittingly came to the rescue: he was in the middle of giving his address, and occasional utterances filtered through to Gareth in a way which seemed to tie in with the issue he was attempting to resolve. 'It was, after all, a question of faith' was one such snippet. Here he was, praying with a desperate fervour he had never experienced before. What he lacked was faith. The question for him wasn't whether he believed God *could* work a miracle, but whether he believed He *would* do so. Megan had stressed the importance of praying really hard. But this was a child's way of thinking; it was comparable to the notion that if you pestered your parents often enough they would relent and give you what you wanted. What difference did it make how passionately he repeated his plea? And would it really matter if he asked ninety-nine times or a hundred? Anyway, what right had he to think that it was within his power to alter the course of destiny? How could he presume to simply turn up out of the blue one evening and persuade God to rescue him from his crisis? Yet Gareth was reluctant to conclude that his efforts were in vain, or that he was powerless to escape his predicament by calling for divine intervention. So he just went on repeating his solitary request until the mental effort required to sustain his inner vision of the divine Being became too much for him.

With a sigh loud enough to cause an old man seated a few rows in front of him to look over his shoulder, Gareth dropped his hands and sat back. The vicar was still exhorting the little gathering to follow the example of their Lord and love their enemies. That, thought Gareth, was precisely what he needed to do. There could be no denying that he had come to see Harvey as an enemy – the only one he had had since his schooldays. If he could only stop feeling this hatred, this bitterness, this deep-seated resentment, then he might be able to keep his problems in perspective. And maybe then God would be willing to answer his prayer. As the service ended, it occurred to him that at least he had something to take away from this episode, and he remained where he was for a couple of minutes and prayed for the strength to love his enemy.

When he stood up to leave, he felt light-headed, and had to steady himself by gripping the top of the seat in front of him. He remembered Andrew's advice that he should eat more healthily - a plea which had been reiterated as recently as the day before. Gareth knew that lack of nourishment was beginning to make him feel weak, but his appetite seemed to have faded even more over the last week. It had crossed his mind that this was connected with the amount of wine he had been drinking, and he had managed to abstain since Friday. So far, however, there had been no sign of an increased desire for food.

Gareth waited until he felt ready to walk steadily before heading home. He would have preferred to leave without having to speak to anyone, but there was no escaping the vicar, who was waiting eagerly by the door. As Gareth approached, however, his smile gave way to a look of concern.

'Good to see you,' he said, as he grasped Gareth's hand. 'Do come again.'

'Thank you,' replied Gareth, and he prepared to continue into the porch.

'Are you new to the area?' the vicar enquired.

'No, I've lived here for some years.'

'Well, you're very welcome.'

'Thank you.' Again he turned to go.

'Wait a second.' The vicar put his hand on Gareth's shoulder and added quietly: 'If there's anything I can do, let me know.'

Gareth nodded. 'That's kind of you. I will.'

But as he passed through the gate he knew that he would not be taking the vicar up on his offer. He had too much pride to turn to a stranger. He would have to deal with this in his own way.

As he made his way back up the hill towards his home Gareth felt a sudden urge to go for a drive.

Chapter 21

On opening the front door Helen felt a shiver running down her back. Certainly the house was colder than it had been when she left it on Friday morning; but it was more than that. There was an eeriness around her which she couldn't quite explain. She had hoped to get back early in the evening, but her flight had been delayed, and the sun had already disappeared into the ocean before she reached Polzeath. Now, as dusk turned to darkness the house seemed unwelcoming, and its surroundings uncharacteristically still and quiet.

Helen put her suitcase down on the doormat and tried to make sense of her unease. Noticing that there wasn't even the slightest hint of a breeze, she decided this would explain the absence of the reassuring sounds of frolicking taking place below. She could not have known that in fact a sea mist had descended onto the beach late in the afternoon, encouraging many of the pleasure seekers to leave early. Some of them would not return to the beach tomorrow, but would be going back to their normal routines. There were just two weeks of the summer season left. Helen knew that the little resort would take on an altogether different character after that.

Leaving the front door ajar, Helen stepped inside the house. As she felt around for the light switch, her mounting apprehension left her in no doubt that she still hadn't entirely shaken off the memory of the burglary. A comment Harvey had made over the weekend had aggravated her misgivings. When questioned about the mysterious message on the answering machine he had revealed that there were several ex-girlfriends who might have wanted to cause him some trouble, especially if they had found out that he had a new lover who had moved in. He told her that it had crossed his mind that the burglary could have been set up by one particular old flame who had never forgiven him for jilting her. Harvey had stressed the need for Helen to be on her guard, and as she entered the dark hallway she shuddered at the prospect of finding that something had occurred while she was away.

Once she had satisfied her self that her fears were unfounded, Helen made a cup of coffee and took it through to the lounge. Only then did she remember to check how Joey was. She had considered asking Andrew to feed the budgie over the weekend, but had decided against this because she knew that it would cause Gareth further anguish if he found out where she had gone. Not knowing anyone else in the neighbourhood whom she could ask, she had left enough food to last for three days and hoped that Joey would refrain from eating the whole lot at once. Helen saw that the seed troughs were empty and wondered how quickly the bird had devoured his supplies. Joey was sitting on his perch, half asleep.

'Poor thing,' she whispered as she leaned over him. 'You've been lonely, haven't you?' She felt glad that the bird's capacity to understand his surroundings did not extend to recognising guilty expressions. 'Are you missing Gareth?' she enquired, and suddenly she felt even more uneasy as she recalled what she still hadn't done. She sighed. 'Now's as good a time as any,' she muttered.

Helen found herself struggling to remember the phone number. Only by talking herself through the digits as she dialled did she become certain that she had got it right. Was her memory that poor, or was it because she felt so nervous, she wondered? When the tones gave way to the call minder she was surprised to hear her own voice. She wondered whether he had simply forgotten to change the message, or whether it was because he hadn't given up hope. Helen was quite relieved that she wasn't going to have to speak to him in person. She didn't know how he might react. Might he have grown to hate her over the past few weeks?

'Oh, Gareth, it's me. Look, I really just wanted to see how you were and to say I'm sorry I had a go at you over that business with Rowena and Jarrod.' She paused, distracted by a solitary chirp from across the room. 'Listen, I really feel we need to talk. I'll be in touch again soon. Look after yourself. Bye.'

As she replaced the receiver she checked the time. It was nearly ten o'clock – surely too late for him to be in the garden. She thought it was unlikely that he would have gone out. Perhaps he just didn't want to be disturbed. Helen wondered whether he would want to ring her back; although she hadn't given him a number he would be able to retrieve it unless someone else called before he got the message. She went over to the birdcage and waited. She sipped her coffee anxiously, while Joey pecked at the toy bird beside him as if to point out that he was hungry, or homesick, or both. The silence remained unbroken, and she returned to

130

the kitchen to wash her cup. Then she realised she hadn't let Harvey know she was back safely. She had remembered in the nick of time that he had promised her the number of the replacement mobile which had just arrived. Retrieving her handset and the tissue on which he had written his new number she set about the task of formulating a message. There was no urgency: he would still be taking curtain calls on the Parisian stage, and might not even check his phone until the following day.

Helen was surprised to discover that there was a message waiting in her Inbox:

'Helen, babe, I'm missing you already. Sorry I was such a pain to you before you left. Will you forgive me? This bloody tour is really doing my head in. I am coming to accept that it is going to be the band's last. I wish you didn't have to stay there on your own. At least it will give you the chance to sort things out. Keep counting the days until I come back. Kisses all over. H.'

She had carried the phone through to the lounge, along with the small pile of post which she had retrieved from the doormat. She flopped onto the sofa and began to sift through the handful of envelopes, her mind was still on the content of the text, and she discarded most of them at a glance. She stopped when she came across some handwriting she recognised. The name and address had been written neatly and carefully using a fountain pen. The style was unmistakably that of her sister Patricia. Normally Helen would have opened the letter straight away, but this evening anxiety restrained her. Helen's concern about the reactions of the rest of her family to her decision to leave Gareth was small compared with her trepidation over Patricia's response. The sisters' rivalry while they were growing up was intense. They had vied for the status of 'Daddy's favourite girl'; they squabbled over dolls, bicycles, and television channels, and later, as teenagers, argued over who would be the first to find a husband. Patricia had a couple of years' advantage in this respect, but had been unable to make them count. It was she who had made Gareth's acquaintance at Hurstpierpoint library, she who had brought him home for tea with the family, she who had hinted about how exciting it would be to go to the barn dances over in Hassocks. It was Patricia who had complimented Gareth on the shrewdness with which he played chess, Patricia who circulated the congratulations card when he passed his driving test at the first attempt, but it was Helen who benefited from the theatre tickets which came his way when Andrew went down with flu, Helen who caught his eye with the minimum of effort. Only now did she fully understand what motivated her when, as a nineteen year old, she had first wriggled free of her summer dress and pulled him to her. The experience might not have been all it was cracked up to be, but it was a prize for which she had competed with her sister, and she had emerged victorious. The same comment applied to the engagement ring which followed later the same year. Ascendancy over her sibling could not be deemed the sole reason for agreeing to marry the young man her father had described at their wedding as 'a fine catch'. Security, together with the eager anticipation of release from the fledgling nest, had certainly weighed more than any notion of love in making the decision. But would she have come to the same conclusion if she hadn't been spurred on by the desire to be the one who was gloating? Patricia had made a valiant attempt to appear pleased for her sister, a façade which would have convinced everyone except Helen herself. As for Gareth, Helen was certain that he had no idea how he had been caught up in the sisters' power struggle, nor of the effect that the outcome had had on his sister-in-law. Only Helen really understood her devastation. She alone knew that Patricia's decision to further her education in America wasn't entirely career-oriented. It was while she was at Harvard that she had met Gerry, a fellow microbiologist, and had lived with him for about five years. Helen remembered the letter through which she had learned of their split. There was little to indicate that it had been a source of heartache to Patricia, and Helen was sure that her sister was still holding a candle for Gareth. She had rarely seen Patricia over the years which followed, and their correspondence had never been more than lukewarm. As Helen sat gazing at the envelope, she tried to prepare herself mentally for the words of condemnation she feared it might contain. She would hardly be able to deny their validity: her loyalty had been to herself, rather than to her husband or to the things their family had held sacred. She had already recognised that, and if Patricia chose to remind her then she would simply have to accept her criticism. At least she could reply that she had decided to act in a way which was in keeping with her true feelings. This thought propelled her into action, and she ripped open the envelope, tugged the single sheet of writing paper free and began to read:

Dear Helen,

Your note arrived yesterday. At first I felt too shocked and saddened to know what to say. But on reflection I am not really that surprised. I always felt in my heart of hearts that you would never be entirely happy with Gareth. But did you really have to leave him for someone you've only just met? Will it be worth it in the end, I wonder? I spoke to Mum last night. She said she was bearing up, but then she would, wouldn't she? I could sense the anger and the disappointment in her voice. She said Dad had gone to bed early with a headache, but I could hear him moving around in the background. I guess he was too cut up to talk. You know he thinks a lot of Gareth. And you know how much I care for him too. I can't bear to think of his pain. I haven't been able to summon up the courage to call him yet. I am flying to Botswana tomorrow, as I am committed to helping with a charity project there. After that I am coming home. If you speak to Gareth, please tell him I will come and see him then. I don't know how long I will be staying for. I have booked my return flight for September 8th but I may try to change that. My work has been getting me down in recent months. They keep placing more and more demands on me and I am coming close to saying enough is enough. So I'm going to look around and see if there are any jobs worth applying for at home. You always said I would come back eventually, didn't you? Well, maybe you will be proved right. You win again, sis!

Do I sound bitter? I try not to be. It doesn't help anyone. I'm sure you have your reasons for your decision. I do want you to be happy, you know. I wish we understood each other better. Maybe we'll get to meet up when I'm home. Anyway, I have to go and pack, as my plane leaves early in the morning, so I'll say bye for now.

Patricia

Helen breathed a sigh of relief. It could have been so much worse. She had always envied Patricia her ability to get her point across, to stand up for what she believed and to influence others. If anyone could have made Helen feel worse about what she had done, it was Patricia. Instead her sister had been quite restrained. However Helen doubted whether there would ever be a real understanding between them. They had too little in common, and too many things had happened to set them apart. Still, she was encouraged that Patricia had expressed an interest in trying to narrow the distance between them. But would she really come back, even if she could find work? It was true that Helen had said many times that she would. But in reality this was because she had secretly hoped that her sister might be encouraged to stay away, if only to prove her wrong. The timing of Patricia's remark was interesting, though. Could it be that she still had feelings for Gareth?

Helen's thoughts returned to the text she intended to send Harvey. She looked again at the message he had sent her. 'Kisses all over' indeed! That was a new expression. But then that was what made Harvey so exciting – his cheek, his freshness, his originality. Yes, he had been a pain to her before she left. But at least he realised it, and was prepared to admit it. As for saying that the tour was likely to be the last, she doubted that he really meant that. Her eyes alighted on the part of the message which had puzzled her when she first read it. What good would being there on her own do? What were these things which she would have the chance to sort out. She dismissed the possibility that he was referring to replacing the items lost in the burglary, or for having a security system installed. Harvey would not have included anything so mundane in a text. If she understood him as she felt she was beginning to, then he had deliberately left the meaning of his statement unclear in order to give her something to think about. Her mind began to churn over their many conversations on the weekend – until suddenly it dawned on her what he could be talking about . . . It was a realisation which made her uncomfortable, even fearful, and one which she would spend the rest of the night examining. By the next morning she would be certain that she had understood him properly. And she would be equally certain of what she had to do about it . . .

Chapter 22

The new school year was due to begin in exactly two weeks, and still Gareth had been unable to start preparing for it. There seemed little hope that the situation would change. He had lost his enthusiasm for work, and knew that without it he would be incapable of performing to the standard required. Indeed, he was coming to the conclusion that he should let the headmaster know about his personal crisis before the start of term, and hope that he would receive a sympathetic response. He had even considered simply sending in a letter of resignation. Perhaps he could find a job which didn't require the same level of concentration, something where he could function on automatic pilot, and complete the necessary tasks despite the impediment of a ruptured heart. He could apply for a job in one of the local factories. If he worked the night shift, he would be able to get by financially, especially now that he did not have to consider Helen, whose tastes were certainly more expensive than his. He reasoned that even if he did encounter money problems, it wouldn't make much difference to his frame of mind. They would just provide him with an alternative source of vexation. Gareth sighed as he rolled over and looked at the clock. It was just coming up for eight o'clock. He wondered what Helen was doing now. She should be leaving for work. Unless of course she was intending to call in on him. He told himself that this was too much to ask. He should be grateful for the message which had been waiting for him when he had returned late the previous evening. He had listened to it several times, enough to know it off by heart. He was longing to find out what it was that she felt they needed to talk about. Did he dare allow himself to see this remark as a sign that there was hope? Could it be that Megan's comment about prayer actually had some basis in reality? It was certainly a strange coincidence that the first contact Helen had made for nearly three weeks should follow within hours of his visit to the church.

Gareth pondered the events of the previous day. He had gone for a drive as planned, hoping that he would be able to take advantage of his sobriety by losing himself in the beauty of his surroundings. It was soon dusk, and he found himself chasing the fading sunlight as he drove towards Newquay. Eventually he acknowledged the futility of this pursuit, and cut inland. Taking each junction as it came, he aimed to get himself lost, in the hope that he would derive some solace from the opportunity to explore unknown territory. He found himself in a place called Goonhavern, which previously had been just a name to him. Here he stopped at a pub, where he drank some orange juice and ate a bag of crisps. Finding a corner in which he could be totally undisturbed, he took the chance to scribble some lines he had managed to put together during his journey. Once again he felt conscious of the need to compete with Harvey. He felt sure that Harvey would write some music for Helen, if he hadn't already done so. It was likely it would take the form of a song. Gareth knew there was no way he could achieve that, but he might be able to come up with a poem – preferably one which told Helen how he really felt and at least dispelled the idea that he lacked passion.

He was pleased with the first two lines:

'These fields of green I despise,

This golden sunlight hurts my eyes'

After that it was a struggle, and half an hour of intense concentration produced just two more lines:

'Ever since you walked out the door,

I can't see beauty any more.'

Hard though he tried, he was unable to think how to continue. He wondered how much it would matter if he never managed to do so. Certainly what he had was better than nothing. Doubtless whatever Harvey would come up with would flow as effortlessly as everyday speech. At least Gareth could justifiably claim that these four lines had been the product of a great deal of thought. Would she really be impressed, or would she just scoff at his efforts? Perhaps she would damn them with faint praise. Concluding that he would ask Andrew's opinion before deciding whether to give it a try, he got back into his car and set off on his travels once more.

Again Gareth took decisions about which way to go on a random basis, until he found himself on the A39 near Wadebridge. From here it would have been a short journey back to Bodmin, but Gareth chose to fend off the signs of fatigue which were starting to press upon him, and continued up the main road, until he spotted the signpost for Widemouth Bay. Arriving in pitch darkness he pulled into the car park at the bottom of the slope. He trudged wearily up the coastal footpath until he reached the point where he had stood on the edge of the cliff a couple of weeks beforehand. Now he chose to examine the part of the terrain which he had likened to a ski slope from a wholly different perspective, looking upwards from the bottom. He tried to convince himself that it was just idle curiosity - he merely wanted to know whether his impression of the potential of this place as a vehicular launching pad was correct. It turned out that the descent was not as steep as it had appeared from above - the angle was perhaps forty-five degrees. Nevertheless it would be sufficient to achieve the result he had previously envisioned. Gareth climbed up to the point where the land flattened out somewhat, and realised that there was considerable space at the top for a car to rest prior to making its run. The plateau on which he was standing was particularly exposed to the breeze. It was surprisingly cold for an August night. This, combined with the cloudy gloom above him, gave the scene an eerier feeling than on his last visit. Gareth had to keep reminding himself that the fascination he was developing with this spot could not lead to anything. He had never been more aware of his allegiance to his brother, who had scarcely allowed a day to go by without sending him some message of comfort and support. Gareth had not seen Jenny at all since her attempt to seduce him, and had only had short conversations with Megan. Andrew had become his only regular contact with the rest of the world, and Gareth wasn't about to do anything which would cause him grief, however desolate his own life might have become.

For many minutes Gareth stayed where he was, ignoring the chill and the fact that he was weary from his endeavours and weak from lack of nourishment. He attributed the pangs he felt in his upper body to the depths of despair into which he was sinking. He continued to strive in vain to extend the verse he had composed earlier. Eventually he felt light-headed and had to squat on the grass for a while, before returning to the car, afflicted by as profound a sense of dismay as he had felt at any time during the whole affair.

He had arrived home after midnight, and was so exhausted that he flopped straight onto the sofa. In his dreams he saw himself once again at the apex of the slope, only this time he was holding a steering wheel. Releasing the handbrake, he felt a sense of peace as his old Ford Escort began to glide down the grassy chute, bumping slightly, gathering momentum as it went. As it sailed out over the edge and began its short flight he was smiling with relief at the sense of imminent release. Even as the vehicle hit the rocks below, exploding on impact, he felt no pain. It was all over in less time than it would have taken for his body to register that it was undergoing instantaneous destruction. And then suddenly he was floating aimlessly above the ocean, looking back on the scene with a sense of satisfaction and accomplishment, free from all the anguish, sensing instead the liberation that comes on entering a new dimension, eager to savour a new state of being.

Waking in the early hours of the morning with a feeling of uncertainty as to his whereabouts Gareth had remembered the dream as vividly as if it had been a real experience, and felt deeply disappointed to discover he was still in his lounge, surrounded by memories of happier times from which he could not escape.

He lay still for a while before deciding to go to bed, in the hope that he might sleep more soundly for the rest of the night. Given the choice, he would simply stay asleep until such time as there was an end to his suffering. He summoned up the energy to get to his feet and staggered towards the door. Passing the phone, it occurred to him to check whether Andrew might have left a message. He was surprised to hear the call minder inform him that there were two new messages. Gareth listened to the first, which was indeed from Andrew, inviting him to call back and let him know how he was. Then he heard the second message, and at once his whole being had been thrown into turmoil. The sound of her voice, the unexpected humility, the hint of lingering affection . . . Everything complemented the impression created by the content of the message that all was *not* lost, and this conclusion so preoccupied him that he hardly dozed at all, even when at around four o'clock in the morning he finally resumed his journey up to the bedroom.

Now as Gareth lay waiting for the digital clock to flick from 7:59 a.m. to 8:00 a.m. he decided to repeat the previous evening's prayer for his wife's return. He reasoned that it could hardly do any harm. But before he had had the chance to gather his thoughts, he was distracted by a sound that was familiar, a dull thud which he had heard hundreds of times over the years, the significance of which had always been the same. The sound was that of a car door being shut. Gareth shot up and hurried round to the front window. Lifting the lace curtain so that he could get a clear view, he scoured the road below in search of the white Fiat. It wasn't where she usually parked it, because that area was occupied by another car. When he looked a little further along, however, he felt a twinge of excitement. He couldn't see her face, or even enough of the car to be sure that it was the right one, but he recognised the grey trousers. Helen was leaning through the open back door of her car, reaching across the seat for something. He couldn't make out what it was, but judging by the way she was struggling with it, it was something bulky or awkward. If he had been dressed he would have hurried down to help her with it. As it was, all he could do was wait and see what it was. When she did reappear, his heart missed a beat. It had not crossed his mind that she could be bringing Joey back, but there he was, fluttering around in his cage. If Helen was returning Joey, then surely she too was coming back. Gareth quickly put on his dressing gown, raced down the stairs, and opened the door. Helen was walking steadily down the garden path. He looked at her, open mouthed, stunned into silence by the suddenness of her reappearance, looking for some indication that his understanding of the situation was correct. He found it in her face. He knew how to spot when she was nervous: she would blink frequently. As their eyes met, Helen's eyelids began to flicker involuntarily. She tried in vain to smile, then looked down at the ground as she took the last few steps towards the front door. She held the birdcage aloft as she stopped just short of the doorstep. Gareth took it, and carefully placed it on the floor just inside the hallway.

It would have been understandable if she had been just a little uneasy about seeing him again, but it was obviously more than that. Helen looked distinctly uncomfortable, as though she were about to learn the result of an important exam. Gareth held out his arms, and after a moment's hesitation she came to him. He could feel that she was breathing rapidly and felt sure that her heart must be racing. The scent which he had gone to such lengths to banish from his system threatened to drive him instantly wild. He pulled away slightly, so that he was holding her at arms length. There was an unmistakable look of sorrow in her eyes.

'So what's all this about?' Gareth asked uncertainly, longing for confirmation that she was coming home, but unable to ask her directly.

'Can I come in?' she asked. Her voice was so soft it was almost a whisper.

He let her go, picked up the cage and led the way into the lounge. Joey was cowering, as though unsure about what lay behind this upheaval. He tilted his head as he looked up at Gareth.

'It's okay, little bird, there's nothing to worry about,' Gareth reassured him. He lifted the cage onto the shelf in the corner, and smiled as he added:

'It's good to have you back.'

He was addressing Joey, but he turned involuntarily as he spoke, so that just as he uttered the last word he caught Helen's eye. He could not have thought of a better way of imparting his reaction if he had tried for weeks.

For a moment, Gareth's remark was greeted with an uncomprehending stare. This changed to a look of horror as Helen made an awful realisation. She sank back onto the sofa and buried her head in her hands. How could she have failed to realise that turning up unannounced with Joey might lead him to make this assumption?

Some seconds passed in silence. When Helen dared look in Gareth's direction she saw only his back. He was staring into the cage, as though focusing on the fact that at least one of his missing companions had returned.

'I'm sorry, Gareth,' she began. 'I mean, I'm sorry you got the idea I might be coming home. I just felt that I should bring the budgie back. I think he's missed you.'

'Huh! At least *he's* missed me. If only you could say the same thing!'

Helen sighed.

'Well, you know me, Gareth. I'm not one for sitting around and moping, or thinking about what might have been.'

'Oh, I see, and I am, I suppose?'

'I didn't mean it like that. Although actually, I do think you're too ready to feel sorry for yourself.'

Gareth turned round but could not bring himself to look at her.

140

Chapter 23

Although he was reluctant to leave the depot in the hands of his new deputy for the first time, Andrew knew his priority had to be to spend time with his brother. After the long phone call the previous day in which Gareth had informed him of the bombshell which Helen had just dropped, Andrew had hardly slept and had gone to work that Tuesday morning intent on getting the essential tasks completed, and briefing his understudy about the things which he would need to oversee during the rest of the week. Andrew's greatest concern was the visit of the internal auditor on Friday afternoon. His deputy was worried that he would not be able to find everything the auditor would want to see, let alone know what it was or whether it was operating efficiently. Andrew hoped that by then he might have raised Gareth's spirits sufficiently to put in an appearance for a while.

Having accomplished everything he could by around six o'clock, Andrew headed for home and hurriedly prepared a meal. While he was eating he gave some thought to what Gareth had told him the night before. Andrew was not surprised that Helen had asked for a divorce, although he had not expected it to happen quite so soon. He wondered whether perhaps she was still hoping to have children. At the age of forty-one, it would not be too late provided she set about it soon. Somehow he didn't see Harvey as a family man – he was too preoccupied with achieving his own objectives. By contrast Gareth would have made a very good father. It was so cruel that nature had robbed him of that privilege. And now his marriage was over, partly as a result of the same misfortune. Andrew couldn't help feeling angry with Helen for accusing Gareth of being self-indulgent. No man, however strong he might be, could be expected to just shrug off such a loss. It wasn't like missing a bus; there wouldn't be another one along in a minute. Nevertheless, Andrew saw an opportunity to help Gareth by encouraging him to think he had to treat the whole experience as a test of his fortitude and resourcefulness, and convincing him that he would have to show a greater degree of determination in order to come through this trial in the end. The biggest problem he foresaw was to convince Gareth that Helen was not worthy of the unconditional and enduring love that he had shown her. It was to this matter that Andrew endeavoured to apply his mind while he tucked into his lasagne. He recalled the glorious day nearly twenty years ago at St. Peter's church in Brighton when they had exchanged their vows. Helen had seemed so calm, so unflappable, apparently so certain that she meant what she was saying. Somehow Andrew had not felt entirely convinced even then that she would be able to fulfil the commitments she was making, but he had felt that it wasn't his place to say so. Did he now regret the fact that he hadn't voiced his reservations beforehand? Would it have made any difference? Perhaps Gareth would have been so blinded by his love for Helen that he would not have taken any notice. And even if Andrew's advice had ultimately affected Gareth's decision to marry Helen, might it not have simply deprived him of two decades of contentment, for which he was only now paying the price? If only Andrew could be sure that his brother would recover from this catastrophic blow eventually . . . There had to be something he could say which would set him on the right road. He simply had to find the right words of solace.

Andrew continued to ponder the problem while he hurried to finish the washing up. He wanted to come back from Bodmin later that evening with the feeling that he had made some progress. It would not be productive to be too critical of Helen, for even now Gareth would not hear a word against her. And if Gareth were steadfast in his loyalty to his wayward wife, then his respect for the pledges he had made to her would be unshakeable. Somehow Andrew had to persuade him that such commitment was only appropriate if it were reciprocated. Andrew recalled that Gareth had readily accepted his assertion that Helen had changed. Suddenly it occurred to him that if he could help Gareth to see that she was no longer the person he had fallen in love with, then he could help him realise the futility of persisting with his devotion to her. And so Andrew reached a conclusion: he must convince Gareth that the adulterous housewife and the naive bride were effectively two different people, and must be treated as such in order for him to move on and make the most of the rest of his life.

Andrew knew it wasn't going to be easy, but he had to believe that it was possible to bring his brother back from the brink of despair. He recalled how a couple of years ago he had spent some time talking to one of the administrators at the depot when he had discovered that his son was battling against drug addiction. The man had moved away since then, but had sent Andrew a letter saying that it was his advice that had helped solve the problem. Although he had no training in counselling, Andrew had a positive attitude, a methodical approach and abundant patience. And now he was determined to do everything in his power to give Gareth the support he needed to see him through this crisis.

As he got into his car Andrew was eager to spend at least a couple of hours at the cottage: that should be enough to make a start on his quest. He checked the clock on the dashboard. It was half past seven. He would be in Bodmin just before eight.

Chapter 24

It was murky in the lounge. Joey was fast asleep on his perch. His owner had been dozing on the sofa, until the clock in the other half of the building had woken him up. He had no idea how many times it had struck. He could see the gloom through the gap between the curtains; but was it dusk or dawn? Feeling too weak to move, Gareth lay waiting to see what happened to the sky. In the meantime, he reflected on Tuesday's events. He had spent the afternoon at the beach in Newquay. He had no particular desire to do so; his only motivation was to honour the promise his brother had insisted he make after Helen had asked for a divorce. Having given his assurance that he would take his mind off his problems by going out somewhere that day, he had forced himself to try to take advantage of the late summer sunshine just as he would have done normally. He had settled near a spot where a tiny island with a single house on top was joined to the mainland by a swing bridge. Usually he would have been quite content to sit and read or have a go at a crossword. Today, however, he hadn't even managed to get sufficiently organised to bring anything with him. Feeling unable to summon up the energy to go into the town in search of a newsagent's, he had decided to make do with an old copy of the North Cornish Times which he had come across in the boot of the car. Soon he found himself seeking solace in the sight of the waves breaking against the distant rocks. Nearby there were youngsters discovering the thrill of exploring the shallow pools. They splashed around exuberantly, yelping and squealing with delight. Gareth's mind was taken back to his own childhood holidays, and to many happy hours spent playing with Andrew. Neither boy had been excessively mischievous. They had mastered the art of self-discipline at an early age, and had learnt to share in a way which would have shamed many adults. Squabbling was a rarity, and good-natured fun very much the norm. As Gareth watched the children at play he couldn't help longing for a return to those days of blissful innocence.

A family arrived and spread themselves out quite close to where he was sitting. At one point a toddler wandered over towards him, apparently intent on showing him a tiny blue spade. A plump blonde lady came running over to retrieve the little boy. She apologised on behalf of her son; Gareth told her it was okay. Pausing for a moment, she looked curiously at him. 'Cheer up,' she said, 'it might never happen.' Gareth shook his head. 'It already has,' he told her forlornly.

Disconcerted at the discovery that his distress was so apparent, Gareth lay face down and closed his eyes. He must have drifted into a deep sleep, because suddenly he was jolted into action by a sharp feeling of coldness around his feet; the holidaymakers around him had all gone, and the tide was coming in rapidly. It was only when he got back to the car that he discovered it was almost seven o'clock. He would have to go straight home in order to be there before Andrew arrived.

The journey had gone smoothly as far as Wadebridge, but shortly after he joined the A389 towards Bodmin he had joined the back of a long queue. He had never been held up on that road before. It was clearly not just the extra traffic which filled the roads in the West Country at this time of year: there had to be either road works or an accident. As he didn't remember passing any road works on the way down, Gareth concluded that an accident was more likely. Soon a police car passed with its emergency lights flashing. Gareth took this as confirmation of his assessment of the situation. The queue had completely ground to a halt; around him vehicles were turning in the road and heading back towards Wadebridge. After some minutes without any sign of progress Gareth conceded that he would have to do the same. Concerned that Andrew would find the cottage empty and be worried, Gareth stopped as soon as he could and tried to call him. There was no answer on his home phone, and the mobile was switched off. As Gareth set the car in motion again, he struggled to contain his irritation. He had to remind himself that whoever was responsible for causing the delay might have much more reason for regret than he had.

Gareth managed to find an alternative route through the country lanes and arrived home just over an hour after he had left Newquay. He was relieved to find that there was no sign of Andrew. Presumably he had encountered the same delay. Perhaps he was held up in the same queue and waiting for the blockage to clear. Exhausted from the exertions of the day, Gareth lay down on the sofa to await his brother's arrival . . .

Several minutes had passed by since Gareth had heard the chimes from next door. He could tell now that the sky was indeed getting darker. It must have been nine o'clock. This realisation gave him fresh cause for concern. Had Andrew really been delayed that badly by the accident?

And why hadn't he rung to explain what had happened? True, he might have left his mobile at home, but would it really have been that difficult to find a payphone?

Getting to his feet, Gareth waited for the light-headedness to clear, and then went across to the front window. Peering through the crack in the curtain, he looked down the row of parked vehicles: his own car, Jenny's Skoda, her friend's blue Vauxhall Cavalier, and a yellow Renault belonging to someone who lived further down the road. Beyond that another vehicle was just pulling away. There would be a space big enough to accommodate Andrew's car if he showed up shortly. Gareth decided to try the phones again. The mobile was still switched off, and the home phone again rang repeatedly until the answer machine cut in. This time Gareth waited for the beeps to finish so that he could leave a message:

'Andrew, it's me. Look, I know you probably won't get this message until after you've seen me. I'm just getting a bit concerned as to where you are. I thought you said you were coming over about eight o'clock and it's gone nine. Can you just give me a quick call to let me know you're all right? Okay, see you later.'

Returning to the window, Gareth was surprised to find that the space was now occupied. The car which had just reversed into the gap was white, but it wasn't Andrew's Mazda. Gareth couldn't see it clearly, but it looked to him like a police car. He drew the curtain back further in an effort to get a better look. As he did so, the door on the driver's side opened and the occupant got out. Gareth could see enough of his uniform to confirm his first impression. A moment later, the passenger door opened and another officer came round the front of the car to join his colleague on the pavement.

Gareth watched as they held a brief discussion. It was difficult to see clearly through the darkness that was settling over the town, but he had a reasonable view of the driver, who was nodding his head occasionally, as though receiving instruction from the other man. Eventually the second officer turned and the two men began to walk in the direction of the cottage. Only now did Gareth become aware of the anxiety that was building up inside him. The expressions on their faces appeared solemn, but the two men lacked a sense of urgency; indeed their pace was almost funereal. They reached Jenny's gate and carried on past it. All at once the

148

combination of circumstances conjured up a hideous new meaning: all the indications seemed to lead to the same unthinkable conclusion. Gareth's stomach was churning as he prayed that they would carry on past the cottage. He looked on in horror as they stopped right by the front gate and examined a piece of paper, as though making sure they had the right address. They looked at each other before proceeding, each appearing to invite the other to be the first to go through the gate.

Gareth could feel the heaving within him. His stomach was empty, but it made no difference. The two men were coming down the path. 'No!' Gareth cried aloud. He left his position by the window, hurried through into the hallway, and flung the door open, startling the policemen slightly as they entered the porch. The officer who had been driving had raised his hand in preparation for the knock at the door: now he allowed it to fall to his side. Gareth's eyes met his, and the policeman realised that somehow this man had already worked out what he was about to be told. He would have to go through the motions, but there was no doubt in his mind: the man before him was indeed Gareth Bell, brother of Andrew Bell, the person whose life had ended in a head-on collision earlier that evening.

If the officer had been surprised by the opening of the front door, and the fact that the intended recipient of the bad news was already in the know, then he was completely unprepared for what happened next. The man before him opened his mouth as if to speak, but instead clutched his stomach and fell to his knees. Then he began to splutter and gurgle in a vain attempt to throw up.

Chapter 25

The waves were crashing down on the jagged rocks, sending up plumes of spray which only just failed to reach a pair of gulls nestling on a ledge half-way up the cliff. The grass on which Gareth was lying as he looked down on this scene was damp from the rain which had fallen earlier that evening. The clouds had gone away now, leaving the stage clear for the stars to glisten. As dusk fell it grew cold, a reminder that autumn was only just around the corner; indeed there were only four more days until the first day of September. Gareth wriggled away from the cliff top, and rolled over onto his back. He cast his eye up the hill to the road. From where he was the terrain above looked even more like a ski slope. It really seemed to have been made for the purpose for which he was contemplating using it. He glanced at his watch: it was nine o'clock. In a few minutes' time it would be exactly one week since the moment he had first learned of his brother's death. On countless occasions since then he had tried to imagine the last few moments of his brother's life. He wondered what had run through Andrew's mind in the couple of seconds during which he would have seen the oncoming van straying onto his side of the carriageway. The police had confirmed that Andrew had been cleared of any blame for the accident; the woman driving the other vehicle, who had escaped with both legs broken, had admitted falling asleep at the wheel. At least his brother had died instantly, Gareth reflected. Would the end be that sudden for him too? The events of the past month had left him in no doubt that he had lost the will to live. But would he really have the strength of mind to do something about it? With his brother's death Gareth's notion that he had a duty to remain in this world had evaporated. Indeed, if he felt any compulsion now, it was to do what was required to be reunited with Andrew and the rest of his family. The option to achieve this was there even as he looked up at the darkening sky. The rocks below were only a few seconds' drop away; yet Gareth knew that he would not be able to step over the edge of the cliff. It was the possibility of using the car which rendered it conceivable that he could make the descent. He would only need a few minutes to go down to the car park, and drive back up to the top. However, Gareth was firmly of the view that now was not the right time.

He had to last until at least Friday, the day of the funeral. It would be unthinkable not to be there. With typical foresight and consideration for others, Andrew had made arrangements for his own interment. He had expressed the wish to be cremated, asked for the memorial service to be kept short, and chosen two favourite hymns, 'Jerusalem' and 'The day thou gavest, Lord, is ended'. He had asked for donations to be made to the NSPCC rather than the purchase of flowers, and had even provided a list of people whom he wanted to be informed of his death. Gareth was sure that his brother had done all this because he had realised how much strain attempting to cope with these affairs would have placed on him, and had been intent on sparing him this aggravation. How fortunate he had been to have been blessed with a brother like Andrew, and how deeply he had felt his sense of loss over the past week. Gareth's isolation was now complete: there would be nobody who would miss him when he was gone. His only concern was what to do with Joey. He did not want Helen to take him back: he felt sure that the bird had not been at home in Harvey's house. He would have to find someone who would take him in and look after him properly. The only other thing he would have to do was write a letter of resignation to the headmaster. He knew that news travelled quickly around Cornwall, but preferred not to leave it to chance for the school to learn of his death. The headmaster and most of the staff at the school had been considerate towards him over the years, and he wanted to make them aware that they would need to find a replacement as soon as possible.

Gareth realised he was starting to shiver, and decided to head back to the cottage. He found that getting to his feet was an effort, such was his weakness from lack of nourishment and sleep. As he stumbled back down the coastal path to the car park, he found himself wondering what he might have done to deserve such a dreadful decline of fortune. His existence had come to feel like a punishment; however, he had not been given a trial, or any indication of his crime. As he reached the car his whole body seemed to ache. It was difficult to distinguish between the pain which derived from his physical debility and that which stemmed from the torment that was devouring him from within. If he were an animal they would have had him put down by now. Somehow this thought prompted a smile, in his mind if not on his face.

As he drove back to Bodmin he became conscious that his head was really beginning to throb. He pulled over into a lay-by on the A39 and tried to rest. Alone in the darkness, he remembered the advice he had been given the previous day. It had come from the policeman who had been driving the car on the night of Andrew's death, who had fulfilled a promise to return and check on his condition. The officer had told him not to try to keep his feelings in check, but to let them come out naturally. 'Now don't you be afraid to cry,' he had said. Little did he know how often Gareth had wept in the few weeks leading up to his brother's death; he had done so even more in the days that followed. And now here he was again, sobbing his heart out as he leaned across the steering wheel, unsure as to the extent to which his grief related to Andrew's demise or Helen's desertion. Pride had prevented him from mentioning his marital problems to the constable, who nevertheless seemed to have realised that there was something amiss apart from the ill tidings he had brought. He had been sufficiently troubled by Gareth's state to ask whether he would like to take the phone number of the Samaritans, an offer which he had declined.

Eventually Gareth pulled himself together sufficiently to drive the rest of the way home, arriving just before midnight. Having said goodnight to Joey, he checked the call minder to see whether anyone had left any messages, as he routinely did when he came home. Now that there was no chance of hearing any words of concern or reassurance from Andrew, he set about this task without any real enthusiasm. Gareth was surprised to discover that a message had been left as recently as 11.30 p.m. He was even more taken aback when he realised that the voice he was listening to belonged to Helen:

'Hello, Gareth, it's me. I've tried ringing you several times this evening, and I haven't been able to get through to you. Presumably you've gone out somewhere. I hope you're okay, or at least bearing up. Look, I will be able to come on Friday. I've asked at work and they said it would be all right, so I'll see you there. Don't bother ringing me back, I'm just going to bed. I'll see you at the church on Friday. Take care. Bye.'

Gareth listened to the message again, then saved it. Somehow it seemed to encapsulate everything which had made him fall for Helen all those years ago. There was warmth and real concern in her voice; it was difficult to believe that this was the same person who had asked him for a divorce a little over a week ago. He was glad that she would be able to attend Andrew's funeral: it would give him a chance to see her one last time.

As midnight struck, Gareth pictured Helen asleep in her bed – or rather in Harvey's bed. In fact, he was only partly right. Helen was indeed in bed, but she was not asleep. She was trying vainly to suppress a thought that she had just had, a thought which troubled her so deeply that it made her whole body feel cold. It hadn't occurred to her before that there could only have been one reason why Andrew should have been travelling on the road to Bodmin the previous Tuesday evening. He was surely on his way to try to help Gareth deal with the latest episode in his tale of woe. If it had not been for her request for a divorce, and moreover for the selfishness which underlay it, Andrew would still have been alive now. In a sense, his death was her fault, and the suffering she would have to endure as a result of this realisation was her punishment.

Although it was too late to change what had happened to Andrew, Helen knew that it was still within her power to come to Gareth's rescue. If she chose to do so she would have to abandon the relationship on which she had pinned so much hope, and for which she had sacrificed her security. It would mean letting Harvey down in the process; she recalled his prediction that she would leave him, and wondered whether his words might turn out to be prophetic. And if she did go back to Gareth, they would both know that her actions had been prompted by sympathy rather than inclination. On the other hand, if she chose to continue to ignore his plight, she would remain riddled with guilt for the rest of her life. The longer she allowed him to suffer, the worse she felt about herself. She had always believed that in order to love other people, it was necessary first to love yourself. Now she was so uncomfortable with what she had done that she no longer loved herself - indeed, she was beginning to hate herself. How then could she truthfully say that she loved Harvey?

It seemed to Helen that there was no way out. She could return to the trap she thought she had left behind her, or she could remain in the trap she had made for herself. It was a simple as that: she had a choice of confinement. This sombre dilemma lurked in the darkness, lingering in her haunted mind well into the night, until eventually Helen succumbed to her exhaustion and was granted a temporary reprieve from her malaise.

Chapter 26

The light was already beginning to fade as a cloudy afternoon turned into a rainy evening. The paper on the empty page before him seemed to have changed to a duller colour in the time Gareth had spent staring at it. He could not be sure how long he had been sitting there, contemplating how to set about the concluding instalment in his account of his forty-two years in the world. He had set himself this task as a way of clearing his mind before embarking on his final journey. So far all he had managed to write was the date: Saturday 31st August. It was entirely coincidental, but it seemed fitting that the end should take place on the final day of the last month of summer. He was grateful that he was not going to have to endure the onset of autumn and winter alone in the cottage, a prospect so bleak that the very thought of it was enough to make him shudder.

Gareth had made up his mind to wait until dusk before doing the deed. He did not want anyone to be around to look on in horror as he took flight. On the other hand he wanted there to be sufficient light to forestall the encroachment of fear. Now that the day was drawing to a close he was eager to complete the work on his journal and be on his way. Exasperated at the lack of progress in this respect he turned back the page and looked for some prompt from the previous day's entry. His gaze fell on the last two paragraphs:

It was typical of Andrew, to have arranged everything so thoughtfully. He must have chosen the crematorium near Cassie's house deliberately, knowing that it would be in her nature to want people to go back there after the service, whereas I would have hated trying to be hospitable at such a time. She seemed to know everyone too, not only those from the choral society, but the people he worked with as well. She must have met them at the functions they had attended. If only she were as reliable as she is good-natured, perhaps things would have worked out between them. It had occurred to me that she might withdraw her offer to provide refreshments when she realised how many people were coming, but she proved true to her word. It was hard, seeing her trying to disguise her sadness, and knowing that she could see mine. She seemed quite alarmed when she saw me and realised how much weight I had lost. She is such a caring person. I hope she finds her soul mate eventually.

I was not surprised that Helen was the first to leave Cassie's. Like me, she didn't know anyone else. And she was finding it all too hard, seeing those women from the depot crying their eyes out, and looking at the wreck that I have become. She left so quickly we hardly had the chance to say goodbye. For a moment I wanted to run after her and tell her that it's not too late to change her mind, that despite everything I would welcome her back with open arms, but I know it wouldn't work. At least I can say that on the last occasion I saw her I behaved with dignity. In truth, I was relieved to get away from Cassie's house as well. I have done most of the things I intended to do now. I have written my farewell letter to Helen, and sent my resignation letter to the school. Now I will finish the rest of the Chardonnay. I will stay sober tomorrow, ready for the drive to Widemouth Bay.

As Gareth reached the end of the passage, he recalled what remained to be said, and flicked the page over in order to resume his task. He paused momentarily to put the light on, before putting pen to paper. Soon the words were flowing:

It was at the funeral that I became certain of what I had to do. I was so surrounded by strangers, I felt like the odd one out. And though Andrew wasn't there in person, he was there in everything that went on. It was as though he were calling me to come and join him, telling me not to be afraid. Now I realise the significance of how I felt when I first came across the slope at Widemouth Bay, in a way that would not have been possible at the time. Before I rejoin those closest to me, I am going to share in their final moments – like Andrew, I will be in a car, yet like our parents all those years ago, I will be sailing through the air.

Am I foolish to think that this is what was supposed to happen, that it was 'meant to be'? If I wanted further evidence, then it is difficult to believe that what happened with Megan on Thursday could be a coincidence. It is odd to think that just as I was looking for a home for Joey, she should have persuaded her mother to let her have a budgie. It is stranger still that on the one occasion when I had seen her since Andrew died she should have thought to tell me about it, and that they were both so willing to accept Joey as their new pet. And if I were still in doubt, then I need only consider the alternative: to stay here, and go through the agony of knowing that Harvey is back and that Helen is with him, and that I will have to spend our twentieth wedding anniversary alone? No, everything indicates that I have made the right decision, and I have no qualms about what I am going to do. There is no point in delaying. Everything is done. It's time to go.'

Gareth put down his pen, and closed the journal. He got to his feet and looked out of the front window at the darkening sky. He felt weak from lack of food, but his mind was strong. His concluding remarks had left him satisfied that he would remain calm when he got to the coast. There was still time for a short rest before he set off. He could at least ensure that the final hour of his life would not be spoiled by physical discomfort. On the other hand he knew that it was important that he should begin his descent in exactly the right place, and that if he arrived in total darkness he might not be able to find the designated spot. So he repeated aloud that it was time to go, and fetched his jacket

Pausing in the doorway of the lounge, Gareth looked around the room to check that he had not overlooked anything. It was as though he were going away on holiday and wanted to make sure he hadn't left anything behind. He had even switched off and unplugged all the gadgets. He had put the television in a black bag: this would be sufficient to indicate that it was useless. Earlier in the day, he had managed to find the energy to tidy up. The letter for Helen was sitting in readiness beside the journal. It was better that she should find it there at a time when the news would have already reached her. If he had posted it, it might have got there before she had learned of his death.

For a moment Gareth tried to cast his mind back to the happy times which had been spent in the cottage. However, these images were soon overwhelmed by more recent ones, bringing on a nauseous feeling which propelled him into action. Closing the cottage door behind him, he headed down the path, passed through the gateway, and got into his car.

Soon Gareth was heading along the A30 towards Launceston; he had decided against taking the Wadebridge road in order to avoid the place where Andrew had died. It was not that he was afraid that this would deter him from bringing his plan to fruition. He simply had no wish to be reminded of the place where his brother had met his end. In fact, far from being scared, Gareth was remarkably calm; indeed he was almost cheerful. He couldn't help wondering, as he turned onto the Bude road, whether this was exceptional amongst people who had decided to take their own lives, or whether it was quite normal to feel a sense of well-being ahead of the moment of release. He was so relaxed he was beginning to feel sleepy. He wondered whether perhaps his body was shutting down in anticipation of its imminent dissolution. He was glad when he reached the coast road. If he had needed to drive any further he might have been forced to stop, as he was anxious to avoid placing anyone else in danger. He had stuck by his resolution to avoid having anything to drink since the previous evening.

Gareth was nearing his destination now. He slowed to allow a vehicle following him to overtake, before carrying on to the crest of the rising ground. Once he was past the apex he pulled over to the side of the road as soon as he could. The journey had taken longer than expected, and it was darker than he had wanted, but he was satisfied that the ideal point from which to begin his descent lay directly to his right. As he closed his eyes to say one last prayer he finally became conscious of his nervousness. Gareth reasoned that he had been concentrating on the driving up to this point, and that this anxiety was a consequence of having stopped. He would be all right once he had set the car in motion again.

He found himself unable to think of anything to say to his Maker. Suddenly it struck him that it was pointless to try to communicate with Him when he was moments away from being in His presence; it was like ringing someone from your mobile phone just as you were walking up their garden path. Gareth was pleased that he was able to make such a light-hearted comparison at such a time: he even managed a smile. It was this moment of unanticipated levity which provided the impetus required for him to turn the key in the ignition.

The road was free of traffic as Gareth began the manoeuvre. There was no pavement to cross, only a kerb to mount. The car wobbled slightly as the front wheels climbed the few inches, the driver's side slightly ahead of the passenger side. The rear wheels made their ascent in unison. As the Escort began to bump across the grass Gareth felt a sharp pain in his chest. It couldn't be indigestion, he thought; there was nothing in his stomach. Again he felt satisfied, this time at the clarity of his thought as the moment of truth loomed. He slowed as he reached the point of departure. It looked just as he had expected it to look. He was about to find out what it was like to be a skier, hurtling down the slope - like Franz Klammer, or Eddie the Eagle. He paused for a few seconds, waiting for the pain in his chest to subside. He didn't want anything to intrude upon the moment.

'Okay,' he said to himself when he was ready, 'here goes.'

Gareth gripped the steering wheel tightly, closed his eyes, and moved his foot across to the accelerator.

Chapter 27

Helen went back to retrieve her sunglasses, then resumed her walk towards the cottage. A stranger stopped her and asked her the time. She knew that: it was nine o'clock - the News had just begun as she was parking. She could have told her the date as well: it was September 3rd, a date towards which she had been counting the remaining days, just as she had told Harvey she would when they were in Paris. Although he wasn't due back until mid-afternoon, she had booked the day off work some time ago, eager not to wait even a couple of hours more than was necessary. But that was before Andrew's death, before her guilt had reached its current height, before the intensity of her excitement had been dissipated. Now, as she approached the gate, she was feeling apprehensive about the two meetings she was going to have that day. It was just over two weeks since she had asked Gareth for a divorce: his response, on recovering his composure, had been to ask her to give the matter a little more thought during the time remaining before Harvey's return. She had agreed to do so, and had indeed agonised over whether this was indeed necessary. She had decided that she would at least give Gareth the opportunity to have his say before coming to a final conclusion.

Helen walked slowly, with her head bowed, not looking to either side of her. She would not have been able to say whether Gareth's car was among those she passed. On reaching the front door Helen rang the bell. She expected Gareth to be there. She had phoned the previous evening, and had left a message saying she would call on him in the morning, adding that he needn't bother ringing back unless her visit would be inconvenient. However there was no response. She went to the lounge window and peered through. The cottage seemed empty. Perhaps he was in the garden. She decided to let herself in.

'Gareth,' she called. There was no answer. She went through into the lounge. Immediately she noticed the empty corner. That was strange; he wouldn't have got rid of Joey, surely? 'Oh, no, don't tell me he's gone and died, as well,' Helen said aloud. Maybe Gareth had gone away, and taken Joey with him. But that wouldn't be right; it was the start of the new term. It dawned on her that some of the schools had gone back today.

Perhaps that was the reason for Gareth's absence. Except that it didn't explain the absence of the budgie.

Looking round the room for clues, she caught sight of her own name, marked clearly on an envelope lying flat on the table. Her reaction was to feel somewhat relieved. Presumably he had heard her message and had left her a note explaining why he wasn't there - although it was odd that he hadn't tried to prevent her from having a wasted journey. She opened the envelope, expecting to find a couple of sentences detailing his whereabouts. It was immediately obvious that the letter was too substantial for that.

Although she started at the beginning, she soon found herself scanning through the paragraphs. She had often complained that his handwriting was too small and difficult to read. He also had a tendency to write at unnecessary length, especially when the subject matter was important. Helen flipped the piece of paper over, to discover that Gareth had completely filled both sides. She was puzzled to see that he had signed it ' *yours forever* ': he had never signed anything that way. Helen resumed her search for the crucial part of his letter. She spotted the words: ' *I don't want you to feel guilty*'. She shook her head, and wondered if he had any idea how guilty she felt. 'That's *not why I'm doing this* ', it continued. Now she began to feel really anxious. 'Doing what?' she asked aloud. Infuriatingly, Gareth's scrawl seemed to grow even more illegible towards the end of the letter. There was a request for her to visit the woman responsible for the accident that had claimed Andrew's life: he wanted her to know he had forgiven her as well. But why couldn't he tell her himself? The awful possibility was creeping into Helen's mind now, although she was doing her best to deny it access: it was out of character, she told herself - Gareth was too sensible to do something as drastic as that. Perhaps he had gone away somewhere . . . The letter was shaking in her trembling hand now. She had to put it down on the table. Only then did her eyes alight on the first few words of the second page: *'will be dead'*. Helen snatched the letter back, made quite sure that her sight had not deceived her, and summoned up the courage to turn back to the beginning of the sentence: ' *By the time you read this I . . .* '

Helen gasped, and threw the letter back down onto the table, as though she had just discovered it had been daubed with anthrax. She shook her head repeatedly. It couldn't be true, she tried to persuade herself. 'I don't believe it. You're not dead,' she called out. But deep down she was uncertain. Suddenly the fact that she had found the cottage empty was more than suspicious: it was creepy. And what's more, it wasn't just empty, it was cold. Over the last few nights the temperature had dropped noticeably. And Gareth hated the cold. If he had been there he would surely have put the heating on. Everything pointed to the same sickening conclusion. Helen swivelled round on the spot, desperately searching for some indication that she might be wrong. She stumbled across to the front window, feeling light-headed now; a suggestion of panic was creeping in. What wouldn't she give to see him coming down the garden path towards her? Helen wondered whether he could see her now. She had heard it said that the spirits of those who take their own lives are unable to find rest, and remain behind in this world in a state of turmoil. She had been told that this was the explanation for phenomena such as ghosts and poltergeists. A macabre thought crossed her mind: was Gareth's spirit even now haunting the cottage? She spun round again, as though expecting to see an apparition behind her. Helen was shivering now, so violently that she found herself holding her arms across her chest in an attempt to gain control. She wanted to convince herself that her speculation was all nonsense. She didn't believe there were such things as ghosts; but somehow she could not deny that it was hideously plausible. He could be right with her now, tuning in to her every thought. It was time to get out of there – but first she had to do something to appease him.

'Gareth,' she whispered, 'if you're listening, I want you to know how awful I feel that things have turned out the way they have. I'm so terribly sorry. I wish I could have felt for you what you've felt for me. The truth is I don't really care about anyone except myself. I'll never forgive myself for what's happened to you. I hope maybe one day you'll be able to forgive me.'

Helen faltered; the cold which was enveloping her was becoming unbearable, freezing the thoughts that were tearing her apart. She didn't dare stay in the cottage a moment longer. She made a dash for the front door, and slammed it behind her as though she were trying to thwart a pursuer. She did not stop to look back as she fled across the lawn, and scrambled over the wall.

Moments later Helen's white Fiat was in motion, going forwards, then backwards, then forwards again before accelerating towards the junction at the end of the road. A driver coming in the opposite direction had to swerve into a gap between two parked cars. His rude gesture was wasted on Helen, who was determined to put distance between herself and the cottage as soon as possible. Within moments she was on the Wadebridge road. She was trying to concentrate on driving, desperately hoping to banish the anguished thoughts which were weighing heavily on her mind. Suddenly any hope of achieving this disappeared as a signpost for Washaway caught her eye. She had forced herself to drive past the scene of Andrew's fatal crash on the way over, but the prospect of doing so again now amounted to a guarantee that still more guilt would be added to her ever growing burden. She decided to look for a different route. Eventually she managed to find a driveway in which she was able to turn the car round. She paused there for a moment, feeling ashamed that she was once more running away. A man tending his garden, irritated by this invasion of his territory, stared disdainfully at her, then relented when he noticed how distressed she looked. With a sigh Helen set the car in motion, and turned back towards Bodmin. As she drove, the notion that she should return to the cottage and try to establish what had happened to Gareth began to press upon her. After all, she was probably the only one who was aware of his intention to take his own life. Perhaps there was a chance that he was still alive somewhere, and that she would be able to save him. She had a couple of minutes in which to think about it. Before she reached the roundabout at the top of the hill, she would have to decide whether to go straight on in the direction of the cottage, or take a left turn into Bodmin and on towards the coast. She could feel the uneasiness building up in her stomach as she contemplated going back into the chilling void that she used to call the lounge, and began to tremble at the prospect that she might find therein something which would confirm that Gareth was dead. What if she drove up there and found she was unable to bring herself to go inside? She would just be wasting time. Surely it would be better to go home, recover sufficiently to take stock of the situation, and then decide how best to set about making some enquiries.

Helen continued to dither as she came up towards the roundabout. Straight ahead was the courageous choice, to the left lay the coward's way out. It was a stark choice, and one she was about to have to make.

Helen gripped the steering wheel tightly, and forgot to change gear. The Fiat stuttered and chugged onto the roundabout. At the last moment Helen turned the wheel abruptly and headed away from the cottage.

Chapter 28

There was a buzz in the air as Harvey came down the hill towards Polzeath. He was reunited with his Jaguar, which had proved none the worse for its stay at Newquay airport. And he had come to a conclusion. The performance he had given in Madrid on Sunday night would be his last with Kosmos. In effect, it would spell the end for the band: they would not be able to function without him. But for Harvey, it would be the beginning of a fresh challenge. Over the weekend a chance encounter with a Portuguese guitarist-composer named Luis had opened up new horizons. There was instant musical chemistry between them, and a song which had been waiting for months for Stig's attention had been completed in a couple of hours. On Monday evening they had met at a bar near the Prado and discussed the possibilities over a succession of tequilas. They had agreed that Luis would visit for a week at the end of September to lay the foundations for a new group. During the short drive home a burst of inspiration had come over Harvey, as though in response to this new creative partnership. As he drove up the hill towards his home he was in a quandary: Helen would be waiting for him, eager to entice him directly up to the bedroom. He knew she had used up a day's leave especially for his return and would be reluctant to accept any delay in having her needs met. On the other hand he could feel a song trying to find its way out of his subconscious; if he didn't give it his attention straight away it might be lost forever. Could he expect her to understand that?

As he brought the Jaguar to a halt on his drive he kept his eye on the front door of the house, expecting Helen to come rushing out before he had even had the chance to open the garage. He was taken aback when this did not occur. Then he remembered that he had sent her a text before he left the airport and that he had not had an answer. One further factor suggested that all was not well: Helen's white Fiat was nowhere to be seen.

Harvey suddenly recalled the prediction he had made the last time they were together. Instinct had alerted him then to the likelihood that she would leave him: now he felt certain of it. All that remained was to find out where she had gone, and why. He knew she had been disturbed by

Andrew's death, but he felt sure that something else must have happened to cause her to abandon ship so abruptly.

There had been many girlfriends who had entered Harvey's life - enough for him to lose count some years ago. It was normal for *him* to be the one who recognised the futility of trying to carry on, usually after a period of two or three months. But there had been a few occasions when he had been the one who was given the push - and he knew how to handle such situations in a way that would keep the pain involved to an absolute minimum. There was no suggestion of anxiety as he put the car away in the garage. So certain was he that Helen wasn't there that he didn't even bother calling her name when he got inside the house. Leaving his cases in the hall he looked around downstairs. He examined the lounge first, to see how it looked without the gadgets which had been lost to the burglar. He noticed how few indications there were that Helen had ever been there. The same applied to the other rooms on the ground floor. There were a few ornaments he didn't recognise, a couple of pairs of shoes which appeared to have been left behind, and some budgerigar food. He saw nothing that would provide him with any clues as to her whereabouts.

Harvey was beginning to feel vexed now. He was still in no doubt that she had left him. He would have hoped at least to find an explanation. And this was happening just at a time when he was about to give life to a really special creation – it would be one of his best songs yet, he felt sure of it. Suddenly a brilliant idea came to him. The tune he had been humming on the way home had a nostalgic, pensive character. Why not add lyrics which reflected Helen's disappearance? It would be better to get to the bottom of it first, though; the song would then capture the full reality of the situation, rather than an incomplete perception of it. Harvey's desire to find out what had happened was redoubled. He was reluctant to call her: he didn't want her to think that he might stoop so low as to beg her to change her mind. With Harvey, there were no second chances; she would not be given the opportunity to leave him again at a later date. In any case he was sure that there would be something around the house which would shed light on the matter. He hadn't checked upstairs yet . . . of course, that was where he should look! It would be typical of Helen to bid her farewell in the room where they had first shared their passion for each other. Still determined not to be fazed by the surprising turn of events, Harvey paused to put the kettle on before heading upstairs.

The bedroom door had been left open; so too had the door of the wardrobe in which hung a number of coat hangers which had not been there when he left. The bed had been left unmade. On the bedside table, propped up by a tissue box, was a yellow envelope bearing his name. Harvey picked it up and took it down to the kitchen. As he made his coffee he promised himself that whatever the contents of the envelope his next action would be to fetch his guitar from the study. With a steady hand, he took out the note and began to read it:

Dearest Harvey,

It breaks my heart to have to tell you of the decision that has been forced upon me. I know you will have worked out by now that I have gone. This morning I went over to the cottage and found a note from Gareth telling me he had taken his own life. I know he wouldn't bluff about something like that. He didn't say how he was going to do it. I cling to the hope that I'm wrong, but in my heart I feel he is dead. Now I feel responsible for his death as well as Andrew's. I am going to have to live for the rest of my life with that awful burden, and I can't see how we could ever be happy now. I would simply drag you down. That's why I have gone, so that I can't do any more harm than I already have. I decided to leave immediately because I was sure that you would try to get me to change my mind. I feel so weak and vulnerable at the moment that I might just have let you persuade me, only to hang around and use you as a prop, and make your life a misery as well. I am going back to my parents' house for the moment. They don't even know I'm coming, or what has happened to Gareth. It's going to be difficult, because they will blame me for everything, but I couldn't possibly go back to the cottage, and there is nowhere else I can go at a moment's notice. I have taken all my most valuable things with me. Anything else you find, you can throw away. If Peterson's ring to see why I haven't come to work, tell them I will be in touch shortly to explain what has happened. I can't face doing it right now.

I think it would be better if you didn't contact me again. My punishment will be to live without you. I know that I will think of you every day for the rest of my life and remember the wonderful moments we spent together. I hope you will soon get over the disappointment and that you will find lasting happiness.

Yours, Helen.

Harvey folded the letter, and put it back in the envelope. In one sense, he felt reassured: at least this did not qualify as a rejection. He placed his empty cup in the sink and carried the envelope through to the study, in case he needed to draw inspiration from it. As he carried his guitar up the stairs to his music room, Harvey pondered the content of the letter. He suspected that Helen's request not to contact her was really a plea for him to do precisely that. Maybe she wanted him to tell her that she should not be so ready to blame herself for Gareth's death. If so, she was taking a gamble – and one which was not going to pay off. However tempting it might be, he was not going to break one of his golden rules. Helen's company had always been enjoyable so far, but he could take it or leave it. In reality it was the sex he would miss; but he would have other lovers, and probably sooner rather than later.

The melody which had come to him on his way back from the airport did not prove elusive. So quick was the flow of the lyrics that at times his hand struggled to keep pace with his brain. Within half an hour he had completed the song, except for an instrumental passage which he would work on with Luis. Harvey looked over his work with satisfaction; he was particularly pleased with the first verse, and the way it led in to the chorus:

There's a special feeling, but it rarely comes, and when it does, it goes,

Once or twice in your life, you will find someone who spins your world around,

Effervescent feelings bubble up within you and you look to the sky as the sun shines in the night,

But it won't last long,

It just can't go on,

You only get up high so that it hurts when you fall down...

Harvey made his way to the bedroom, and looked out of the window. It was late in the afternoon, and the sun was getting low in the sky: the line where the sky and the sea met was a blur. The evenings had drawn in appreciably since he had last spent a night in his new home, and the number of surfboarders and bathers bobbing in the water had dwindled as soon as the season had ended. Harvey sighed, and rubbed his tired eyes. He examined his fingers and noticed a trace of moisture. He wanted to blame this on the effort of concentration required to write his song. He did not want to admit to having to acknowledge sorrow over the loss of a woman.

It had somehow occurred to Harvey while he was composing that he ought perhaps to feel guilty about Gareth. But he didn't. Gareth had allowed himself to become too dependent on Helen. That was *his* mistake, and Harvey was not going to accept responsibility for the consequences.

Turning, Harvey saw the unmade bed, and paused. He would change the sheets straight away; then he would gather up the other things that Helen had left behind, and bin them. This was another of his policies for handling break-ups: get rid of the reminders as soon as possible. Right now he had to admit to being a little downhearted, despite the triumph of the song. But by tomorrow he would feel better, and by the day after he would probably be back to his normal self. Right now, if he closed his eyes he could see Helen's image perfectly. The time would come when he would struggle to picture her at all.

Chapter 29

There were several parked cars in the immediate vicinity of the cottage, but Patricia saw that it would just be possible to squeeze the black Mercedes into a gap outside the other half of the building. The journey from Bournemouth would have been even swifter if she hadn't stopped several times to try to see off her headache. On her arrival at the airport she had been hit by the difference in temperature compared to the States. Now as the electric window sank into the door the chilly air which drifted into her father's car confirmed that the West Country was no more welcoming in that respect. Craning to see how far away she was from the vehicle behind, Patricia noticed that the throbbing in her neck, which appeared to have relented, had returned with a vengeance. She disliked taking tablets unless she had to, but as she brought the car to a halt she conceded that she would have to ask Gareth for some aspirin. She sat back and began to massage the painful area for a few moments, eager to put her discomfort to the back of her mind before she went into the cottage. It had been five years since her last visit, and she was a little apprehensive about seeing Gareth again. She felt sure he would have changed, and that the strain of the past month would have taken a severe toll on him. She would take him in her arms and hold him to her, let him stay there for as long as he wanted, be his comfort and his consolation in his hour of need. As she rolled her head in an attempt to make the pawing movements of her fingers more effective, she noticed that she was being watched. A little girl's face was visible over the wall to her left. Patricia smiled at her, and dredged the depths of her memory for the name of the toddler whose acquaintance she had made very briefly back in '97. The girl turned away, as though she had been caught out, then looked back again and grinned awkwardly. Somehow this provided the impetus for Patricia to take the final steps of her journey. She decided to leave her suitcase in the car until she was sure it would be all right for her to stay in the cottage. Although Gareth had once assured her that she was welcome to stay any time, this was the first occasion on which she had turned up without checking first. Patricia couldn't count on Helen to have relayed the message that she was intending to visit. What bothered her was that when she had called Gareth last night, and again this morning, to let him know she was coming, she had not managed to obtain an answer - despite the fact that she had left messages asking him to return her call as soon as possible. Had he gone away somewhere? If so, she had some numbers for local guesthouses: she would book in for the night and resume her quest in the morning. Or was he really in such a bad way that he couldn't bring himself to speak to her? Could it be that he was trying to protect her from what she would come across? As she came round the front of the car she braced herself for what she might be about to find.

The little girl had come to her front gate, and was resting her chin on its apex.

'Hello, what's your name?' Patricia asked as she approached.

'Megan. M-E-G-A-N,' came the reply.

'I remember you. You were about two years old when I last came to stay.'

The little girl was eyeing her warily.

'You look like Auntie Helen.'

'I'm her sister.'

Megan nodded:

'She doesn't live here any more.'

'I know. I've come to see Uncle Gareth.'

'Mr Bell's not been very well.'

'I know, dear. I've come to help him get better.'

This brought a smile to the little girl's face: she was satisfied that the new arrival's resemblance to her sister was only visual.

'Have you seen him recently?' Patricia asked.

Megan gave the matter some thought:

'Not today,' she began. 'Not yesterday,' she added positively. Then her expression became more vague:

'It might have been the day before.' She shrugged her shoulders and looked apologetic. 'Or maybe it was the day before that.'

Patricia thanked her and moved on through the adjacent gate. As she made her way down the path towards the front door, Megan skipped

170

across the grass until she reached the fence, hoping to share in the excitement of the moment of reunion.

Patricia knocked and waited for a response. She glanced nervously at Megan, before trying again, louder this time.

'He must have gone away,' she concluded; but Megan was shaking her head.

'His car's there,' she said.

Patricia turned and examined the row of vehicles in the street. She was struggling to remember what car Gareth had been driving last time she had come over. Megan was pointing to a red Ford Escort, with a buckled bumper and a dented grill. Patricia nodded her head slowly: she was convinced it was Gareth's car. She squinted as she tried to comprehend the nature of the damage to the front of the vehicle. Soon after her arrival her parents had given her the shocking news of Andrew's death. Had Gareth been involved in an accident as well? She felt renewed determination to get to the bottom of things right away.

'Does your mum have a spare key?' she asked Megan.

'I don't know. Mummy's upstairs at the moment. She's asleep.'

Patricia hesitated:

'I'll try getting in round the back.'

The side gate was shut, but not locked. There was a line of pot plants along the edge of the path at the back of the house; the flowers in them had been left to wilt. By the time she got to the back door Megan was waiting for her on the other side of the hedge.

Patricia turned the handle and the door opened. She glanced uneasily at Megan before going in.

Finding the kitchen empty, Patricia made her way into the lounge. As Helen had done before her, she immediately noticed the cold, as well as the murkiness that accompanied the autumnal evening. She too was left with the impression of dereliction. She went to the bottom of the stairs, and called Gareth's name, realising as she did so that she did not expect to receive an answer. Feeling certain that something was wrong, she made her way up the stairs. She paused on the landing, and called him once again; there was no need to raise her voice this time. Still she was greeted by silence. The bedroom door was slightly ajar. With mounting apprehension she pushed it open and peered round. The duvet was a heap in the middle of the bed. Was it possible he was underneath it? Gingerly she took a handful of the fabric and tugged. The duvet came away from the bed easily to reveal a sheet which had been fitted over the mattress poorly; one corner had slipped off altogether. Patricia moved on to the spare room. Someone had made the bed, in feminine colours. She wanted to believe that Gareth had been the one who had done this, in anticipation of her visit, but she was forced to admit that it looked too tidy to be his handiwork. Surely it was a legacy of Helen's final days in the cottage. A musty smell suggested the room had been left untended for some time. Domesticity had never been one of Gareth's strong points. How likely was it that he would have attended to the housework, given his state of mind? Patricia felt a wave of anger towards her sister, and she became even more determined to find Gareth as soon as she could, despite the fact that darkness was beginning to fall and the pain in her head was sharper than ever. For the sake of thoroughness, she checked the bathroom before going back downstairs. There were no clues in there; nor were there any remedies for her headache in the cabinet above the basin. Patricia concluded that she would have to get Megan to wake her mother up and find out whether she knew anything.

As she came back down the stairs, she noticed some items of post protruding from the letterbox. She pulled them free and examined them. There were three envelopes: all were official in character - bills or junk mail, nothing private. There was one day's post there, maybe two: Gareth could not have been absent for very long. She took them through to the lounge, and put them on the table. Although the room was even gloomier now, there was enough light for her to notice the envelope bearing Helen's name. Further along the table she could see the crumpled sheet of writing paper which had obviously been taken from it. Nearby lay a book: the handwriting which filled most of the page at which it had been left open was recognisably Gareth's.

Patricia hesitated for a moment and considered her right to examine these discoveries. Instinct told her that the letter would be more informative, but she was reluctant to read something that was intended for her sister and which was certain to be deeply personal. Her interest in its content was not due to idle curiosity, but to her grave concern before a very perplexing situation; yet she was conscious of the possibility that either

172

Gareth or Helen might take exception to the fact that she had looked at it. She decided on a compromise: she would not read it thoroughly, rather she would sift through it for anything which might give some indication of Gareth's whereabouts, and do her best not to take in anything which was not relevant. Her head was really throbbing now, but as she picked up the note it was her anxiety which was troubling her most. Patricia checked the date of the letter: 30th August - that was last Friday. She was encouraged to see that he had been well enough to express himself on paper as recently as that. She began to scan through the sentences which followed. Her eyes picked out various phrases: ' *take anything you want from the cottage . . . give the journal to Megan when she has grown up . . . I only want a short and simple service . . . .* ' Each phrase meant little on its own, but when put together their undertones were ominous. Abandoning her attempt at selectivity, Patricia scrutinised Gareth's tiny handwriting for anything which would contradict the impression his statements were giving her. Finally she came to the words which had affected Helen so profoundly: ' *By the time you read this I will be dea*d'. The statement hit her with the force of an electric shock, aggravating the piercing sensations which were wreaking havoc under her cranium. 'No,' she said aloud, 'I don't believe it.' Patricia was not one who admitted defeat easily. Gareth's absence from the cottage, his failure to respond to her calls, and now this letter with its devastating implications, were evidence, but they were not proof. She returned to the letter, and examined it until she was satisfied that there was no reference to the means by which Gareth had intended to kill himself. She thrust it aside and turned her attention to the book, which she realised immediately must be the journal Gareth had mentioned. The first thing that struck her was the date: Sunday 1st September. The most recent entry was just two days old: that meant there was hope! She clasped her hands together as though in prayer as she began to read the paragraph before her:

So it's the first day of a new month - and a day I never expected to see. It's hard to believe I'm still here. I thought I knew myself well, that I possessed the resolve required to finish what I set out to do. How wrong I was, and how disappointed I feel with myself now that I know that. I've been over what happened time and time again in my mind, hoping to persuade myself that it was that rock that stopped me - the rock that seemed to have been put there specially to wedge itself under the car. But I can't deny it. I know I had already switched my foot over to the brake,

173

and without the rock's intervention I would probably have ended up at the bottom of the valley, with a wrecked car, but alive all the same. I keep accusing myself of cowardice, of being irresolute, and of being a weakling. I felt even more hopeless when those two men came along with their dogs this morning. They just lifted the car so effortlessly. I don't know whether they believed what I told them. I suppose it's possible that I could have pulled off the road to admire the view and forgotten to put the handbrake on. Many times during those awful hours spent alone in the darkness, in such pain and distress, I wished I could have another try. I really believed that if I could I would not hesitate this time. But now I wonder whether that was true. If I was so determined to do it, I need only have walked down to the cliff top. Maybe I was fooling myself all along. But I do remember the moment which made me falter, and what it was that caused me to hit the brake, and I will try not to think too badly of myself because of it. In a way it was strange that I had not had the thought before. I had presumed that since Andrew died there was nobody who would have cared that I should have chosen to bring about my own end. Suddenly I thought about little Megan, and how it might seem to her, perhaps not now, but as she grows up, and in particular once she is old enough to understand my account of the past month, and the events which led me to take such drastic measures. Now I curse whatever whim made me decide to ask Helen to give this journal to Megan, for without it I might never have had the thought which brought about the undoing of my plan, and returned me to this miserable existence which can hardly be called a life. And if the traumas that have affected me so deeply were not sufficient to make me regret that my ordeal has been prolonged, I now find myself fighting a new affliction, the onset of which coincided with my arrival at the cliff top. What is the significance of these pains which jab at my chest in short bursts and then go away again? If I wanted to be cured I would have called a doctor by now. But in truth I see them as a source of fresh hope. I hope that this heart which has ached so much in such a short space of time is about to give out altogether. For in reality I feel that this extension to my sentence will not last indefinitely. It is as though all life has gone from me already, and it is just a matter of time before my body finishes catching up. I only hope the process will not be a long, drawn out one, and I pray that I will not go back on my intention to endure this new form of suffering and allow it to take its course, with no remedies other than a few bottles of Shiraz or Jacob's Creek. I have enough wine to last until tomorrow; if need be I will have to fetch some more in time for the day after, the dreaded day when my heart's desire will be reunited with her lover, the day I hoped I would not live to see . . .

Patricia stood still in the silence of the dusky room, trying to reconcile her confused emotions. Her relief at the discovery that Gareth had not succeeded in taking his own life had given way to renewed anxiety about his well-being and the fact that there was still no indication of his whereabouts. The abrupt ending to the narrative added a further dimension to the puzzle. She flicked back through the pages leading up to the most recent entry, not really knowing what she was expecting to find, merely hoping to spot something which would give her some clue as to what to do next. She noticed that Gareth had made some sort of entry, however brief, every day. It was strange, then, that there was nothing at all for the previous day, Monday 2nd September.

Placing the journal back on the table, Patricia looked helplessly around her. She was left with an uneasy feeling, but no idea as to where to turn. She wondered whether she should call the police, and report a missing person, but for all she knew he might simply have gone to the off-licence to stock up with wine. Deciding it would be better to make some more enquiries first, Patricia went back through the kitchen. Megan was peering over the hedge, and was clearly eager to pass on a message she had been given:

'Mummy says he's in the garden.'

For a moment Patricia looked at her, uncomprehendingly. Then she turned and peered into the gloom, trying to make out whether any of the dark shapes towards the bottom could be big enough to conceal a human form. Before she could come to any conclusion, she heard the sound of a window opening somewhere above and behind her. Looking up, Patricia could see a face she vaguely recognised as belonging to Megan's mother. Jenny pushed the window further open and craned her neck. Patricia could see the anxiety in her expression. Her eyes were trained on the far end of the garden.

'Go right down the bottom!' Jenny called, as Patricia began to pick her way down the path, passing the rose bushes with their shrivelled heads, stepping over the weeds which had been allowed to encroach on the stone slabs. The evening mist, seeping in from the moor, made it difficult to see the foot of the garden. She could tell that there was nobody on the bench. As Patricia got closer she reached a point where she began to see through the undergrowth immediately beyond it. Suddenly she thought she saw a face.

'Gareth?' she enquired weakly. There was no reply. Patricia plucked up the courage to move on a couple of paces. Now she was able to make out a crumpled shape, huddled against the wall. There was no doubt that it was Gareth. The realisation that he had to be sitting upright spurred Patricia on; but first she closed her eyes for a moment, and prayed that she would find him alive. She was suddenly oblivious to the awful pain in her head. Using the overgrown hedge to her left for guidance, Patricia carried on down the path until she reached a point from which she knew she would be able to see him properly. Only then did she open her eyes.

Gareth's head was tilted forwards at an angle, and his hands were spread out on the ground on either side of him. Patricia tried to see whether Gareth was breathing, but in the gathering gloom she found it impossible to tell. She edged closer, bent down over him and whispered his name. Gingerly she took hold of his arm and felt for a pulse. His head rolled sideways and his mouth fell open. Startled, Patricia let go of his arm. Somehow she found the courage to kneel down on the hard paving stones and look closely at him. Suddenly, she realised that his chest was rising and falling.

'Gareth, wake up!' Patricia urged. She reached out and caressed his cheek. At last he opened his eyes and stared at her, uncomprehendingly. A wave of relief swept over her. Gareth was looking around, as though trying to make sense of the fact that he was surrounded by pots and bushes. He began to struggle into an upright position. Seeing how weak he had become, Patricia placed her other hand on his chest to prevent him.

'It's okay, stay just as you are,' she said calmly.

He did as she requested, and took a deep breath. She smiled at him reassuringly. Eventually he managed to speak.

'Patricia. It's . . . it's . . . good of you to come,' he said warmly. 'I just wish you hadn't found me like this.'

'How long have you been here?' The concern in her voice was obvious.

'Well, I guess I must have been here since yesterday, at least,' he replied. 'I . . . well, I reckon I fainted. I remember feeling very light-headed. And I remember being conscious for a while and it was cold and dark.'

'Are you hurt?' Patricia asked.

'I don't think so,' he responded. 'I can't feel anything. You know, when you woke me up just now I thought I was dead.'

'I thought you were dead too.' Patricia shook her head in dismay. 'You're so pale and you've lost so much weight.'

'I never thought anything could have affected me like this. I must look awful to you. Please don't think badly of me.'

Patricia took Gareth's hand and squeezed it gently.

'I'm going to call an ambulance,' she said firmly.

'Oh no, don't bother, there's no need.'

'But you're in a bad way. You're suffering from malnutrition. If I hadn't found you here this evening, who knows how long you would have lasted?'

'Okay, I guess you're right,' Gareth conceded.

Patricia went to stand, but Gareth kept hold of her hand.

'Wait! You haven't told me why you're here.'

She paused before answering.

'Well, I was coming to visit anyway.'

'Have you been back long?'

'I just arrived this morning.'

Gareth looked earnestly at her.

'And you've come straight down here to see me?'

Patricia nodded.

'I've come to undo the harm my sister's done.'

Gareth thought for a moment.

'You're an angel.'

Patricia smiled.

'No, no, I'm not an angel.' She squeezed his hand again. 'It's just that I care about you,' she said softly. Then she looked him in the eye, and added, 'I always have.'

They held each other's gaze for some moments, without speaking, until Patricia remembered that Megan and Jenny were waiting anxiously for news of Gareth, and that she ought to go and put them in the picture. When she finally broke away, Patricia felt confident of two things: given time, Gareth was going to recover; and when he was better, he was going to find out what it was like to be truly loved.

About the author:

Mark Tournoff was born in Aldershot, Hampshire in 1962. He was educated at Lord Wandsworth College, near Basingstoke. He studied Theology at Exeter University, and later Management Accountancy at Croydon Business School. He has worked in the Civil Service, the Health Service, and the transport industry. He has travelled extensively within the United Kingdom and on the continent. His decision to become a novelist followed a course of study with 'The Writing College'. His first novel 'A Nightmare in *Paradise*' (Forestdale Publications ISBN 095450720-7) was published in July 2003.

Mark has made many appearances on Channel 4's popular quiz show 'Countdown', of which he was overall champion of series 54 in December 2004, as well as runner-up in the Champion of Champions series 12 in June 2006. He also won the maximum prize on Channel 5's 'Brainteaser in April 2005. His interests include playing the flute in the Croydon Symphonic Band, singing, golf and badminton. He has previously written flute music, songs, sketches and short stories.

Printed in the United Kingdom
by Lightning Source UK Ltd.
116776UKS00001B/10-75

9 780954 507213